"HE STOLE MY HORSES. I GOT A WITNESS."

"Whatever happened to your horses last night, Billy Franklin didn't see it," the sheriff said coldly.

Slocum half rose from his chair just as the back door he had looked to for sanctuary clattered open. Two men stood outlined in the doorway, the bright sun behind them. They had rifles leveled and were ready to start shooting.

"You say the word, Pa, and we'll take care of them."

"Walter and Charley Goode," McDonald muttered under his breath. He stood, hand on his six-shooter and ready for serious fighting. Slocum kicked away his chair and stood also, not sure any of them would survive the cross fire set up by Goode and his sons.

JAKE LOGAN

THE AZTEC PRIESTESS

JOVE BOOKS, NEW YORK

THE AZTEC PRIESTESS

A Jove Book / published by arrangement with
the author

PRINTING HISTORY
Jove edition / September 1997

All rights reserved.
Copyright © 1997 by Jove Publications, Inc.
This book may not be reproduced in whole
or in part, by mimeograph or any other means,
without permission. For information address:
The Berkley Publishing Group, 200 Madison Avenue,
New York, New York 10016,
a member of Penguin Putnam Inc.

The Putnam Berkley World Wide Web site address is
http://www.berkley.com

ISBN: 0-515-12143-6

A JOVE BOOK®
Jove Books are published by The Berkley Publishing Group,
200 Madison Avenue, New York, New York 10016,
a member of Penguin Putnam Inc.
JOVE and the "J" design are trademarks
belonging to Jove Publications, Inc.

PRINTED IN THE UNITED STATES OF AMERICA

10 9 8 7 6 5 4 3 2 1

THE
AZTEC PRIESTESS

1

John Slocum took off his dusty black Stetson and wiped a river of sweat from his forehead. The fiery New Mexico sun was hotter this summer than he could ever remember. The Rio Grande, miles off to the west, was a mere trickle, hardly worth following along the Jornado del Muerto, the Journey of Death, all the way north to Santa Fe. He had no real reason for heading there, except it wasn't El Paso, where he rode from.

He wished he had already arrived in the sleepy territorial capital of adobe buildings and crooked politicians. Anything to escape the Hell of wherever he was now.

He patted his sorrel's neck. "Not too smart traveling in the middle of the day," he told his sturdy horse, "but Tularosa has to be around here somewhere."

Slocum had seen a battered sign along the twin ruts that passed for a road several miles back declaring Tularosa to be ahead. He knew any tracks left on the hard, sunbaked ground wouldn't give much of a clue about other travelers. The dry alkaline dust swirled around his boots as he trudged along, giving his tired sorrel a rest from carrying its heavy load.

"Need to find some water, but there's nothing but mesquite and greasewood around here. No springs likely. Not even a hint of water pooling around a cottonwood." He snorted in disgust. There weren't any cottonwoods.

Slocum turned his green eyes toward the Sacramento Mountains, and knew water flowed free and easy up there. Years back he had explored those hills and found one fresh spring after another, but now he had to decide between a very long trek into the cooler mountains or continuing along the monotonous road and enduring the bitter taste the dust left in his mouth.

How far to Tularosa? Or should he head into the green mountains and find some respite from the punishing sun?

"Whiskey," Slocum decided. "Tularosa has to have a saloon or two willing to sell me a bottle." He tried to spit, but his mouth had filled with gummy cotton. He wiped his lips across a dirty sleeve and kept walking. His horse whinnied in protest, but Slocum was anxious to get to shade. If there had been even one decent tree in sight, he would have gone to earth and waited for the sun to set before plodding on.

There wasn't.

An hour later Slocum thought he might be seeing a mirage, but no mirage carried with it the smell of several hundred people and the way they lived. His nose wrinkled at what the sun did to outhouses and horse dung and even the people, but he had never smelled anything sweeter. Slocum picked up the pace, walking his horse toward a rundown stable at the edge of Tularosa.

"Tend her real good now, you hear?" he told a towheaded

boy. The boy deftly snatched the dime Slocum tossed him.

"Fifty cents is the going rate," the boy said. "Per day, but we give grain and not straw like that good-for-nothing Bert Connelly at the other end of town."

Slocum had to smile. The boy couldn't be more than ten and already had learned business guile from his pa.

"Here's a dollar. Reckon I can last in Tularosa for a day or two to rest up."

"Powerful long way to Santa Fe," the boy said. " 'Less you're heading west."

"How about east?"

"Nothing there. Nothing in Santa Fe, for all that, but since you came up the road from El Paso, I figured you was headin' north."

"Curry her and see if the front shoe is coming loose," Slocum said, deciding the sorrel was in good hands. The boy seemed to know horses as well as business and had a good mind.

He walked slowly down the boardwalk, staying out of the burning sun as much as he could. He had fried his head long enough for one day. All he wanted now was a drink and a soft bed under him. Gambling in El Paso had been profitable until the meddling marshal, Dallas Stoudenmirer, had chased him out. Slocum had tried bribing the lawman and had been sent packing.

"Wasn't even cheating," Slocum grumbled. Not that he wouldn't have resorted to a little deck stacking if the need arose. The gamblers in El Paso had been so piss-poor he hadn't needed to do any double-dealing. Not a one of those at Slocum's green felt-covered poker table at the Gored Ox Dance Hall had ever learned odds or how poorly it affected their gambling if they drank too much.

Still, he had well nigh a hundred dollars in winnings to get him north. After Santa Fe, maybe Denver could be a place to winter. Slocum chuckled at the notion of wanting a place to hide away from the heavy snows of mid-January. It was so hot right now he was melting into a puddle—and one without a whole lot of liquid in it.

Pushing through the swinging doors of the El Greco Saloon took him into a world hardly cooler than outside but infinitely dimmer. He inhaled deeply, and his mouth began to water for the first time all day. At the long wood bar he found a free lunch waiting for him, along with a bottle of rotgut that had a poorly printed label plastered on it proclaiming its origins in Kentucky.

A single sip convinced Slocum it had been concocted in the back room of the saloon out of gunpowder and rusty nails to give the raw alcohol body and color, but he hardly cared. It was wet, and it had the kick of a goosed mule.

The ten dollars for the bottle struck him as steep, but Tularosa didn't see many travelers. He didn't begrudge the barkeep his profit, not when the food that came along with the whiskey settled peacefully into his grumbling belly.

"The way you're wolfing down that food makes me think you been on the trail for a long time," the barkeep said. He idly polished the glasses, missing spots and not much caring. The saloon was deserted except for Slocum and a man in the far corner nursing a drink.

"Been a spell," Slocum said between mouthfuls. "Any jobs in these parts?" He didn't care if there were, but thought this was a way of keeping the barkeep occupied and away from asking questions that weren't to Slocum's liking.

During the war Slocum had been a captain with William Quantrill and his bloody-handed guerrillas. After the Lawrence, Kansas, raid he had been gutshot for protesting the brutal way every man and boy more than eight years old had been cut down, armed or not. It had taken him months to recover his strength, and when he'd returned to Slocum's

Stand back in Calhoun, Georgia, he'd found his parents dead.

Tending the farm had proven a double chore, with his brother Robert killed during Pickett's Charge and memories lurking in every room of the small farmhouse. Worse had been the carpetbagger judge who had taken a fancy to the farm, thinking it would make a good stud farm.

Taxes? Never paid, the judge had said. Slocum had known better. The farm had been in the Slocum family since George I had deeded it over a century earlier, but he hadn't protested. He had seen how Reconstruction politics worked, and when the crooked judge had ridden out to seize the farm, bringing along his hired gunman, Slocum hadn't put up much of a fuss.

Fact was, he hadn't argued one bit. He had simply cut the arrogant scoundrel down where he stood, along with the too-slow gunman at his side. Then Slocum had ridden off, leaving behind two fresh graves up near the springhouse. Since that day, wanted posters had dogged Slocum's every step. Even if the thieving carpetbagger had gotten what was coming to him, the law didn't abide judge-killers. Slocum had seen some posters with rewards as high as two hundred dollars, a powerful inducement for most men simply to shoot him in the back.

Best to keep the barkeep talking about local matters and not get into asking questions Slocum wanted to avoid.

"Well, now, you got the look of a cowpuncher about you, I reckon," the barkeep said. "There's the Stuart brothers' spread out near Coyote Springs. Over yonder is their foreman, George McDonald. A good man, George. He gets a bit morose at times, but he is engaged to about the prettiest little filly in these parts."

"Do tell," Slocum said, finishing a sandwich and wondering if he ought to fix another. He took a long pull on the bottle and let the fiery liquor wash down the remainder of the bread.

"Nettie Fry. Her uncle's none other than Oliver Lee, the finest soul what ever walked this planet."

"But they're not hiring," Slocum said, reading between the lines.

"Nope. Purty near everyone wants to work for them. Then there's John Goode."

"But he's not hiring either?" Slocum asked, curious as to the tone in the bartender's voice.

"Can't rightly say. He's one mean Texas son of a bitch, and I hope he fries in Hell!"

"Wouldn't work for a man like that," Slocum declared. "Rather push on north and see what Santa Fe has to offer."

"Smart thinking," the barkeep said, relaxing. "Goode's anything but smart. He and his family breezed in from central Texas a year back and act like they own the place. Conceited, thinking they're better than the rest of us. Give 'em a wide berth."

"Consider it done," Slocum said. He glanced over his shoulder at George McDonald. The man had bathed recently and had a haircut and shave, as if he was going courting. His threadbare clothes were clean enough too, and he had on good boots, the hand-tooled sides gleaming in the dim light of the saloon.

"Would he mind if I sent him a drink, sort of wishing him the best with his forthcoming wedding?" Slocum held up the remainder of the bottle. He was a little tipsy, but the way the liquor sloshed in his belly told him he ought not finish the bottle, as much as he wanted to. Plain water would serve him and his dried-out body better.

"George is a polite man. I think he'd look kindly on such a gesture." The barkeep smiled, glad to see that Slocum had accepted his version of how things were around Tularosa.

Slocum didn't much care if McDonald was in league with the Devil. All he wanted was to move on and, somehow, the whiskey remaining in the bottle was proving to be a barrier to that hankering.

Slocum walked over and placed the bottle on the table beside McDonald. The man looked up, his expression unreadable. He had pale blue eyes that might have been cruel but instead were only distant. A small scar on his cheek had puckered and turned pink rather than the more usual white, giving him the look of a poorly sewed-up doll.

"The barkeep said you were foreman of the Stuart brothers' ranch, and that you were getting hitched soon."

"What's it to you?"

"I'd like to drink to your good fortune," Slocum said, pushing the bottle over.

"You ain't with Goode and his boys, are you?" McDonald's eyes darted from Slocum's face to the worn ebony butt of the Colt Navy in the cross-draw holster. It was obvious that the side arm had seen hard use, and that Slocum was deadly expert in the way he used it.

"Never heard of him—or you—'fore I stepped into the saloon," Slocum said. "I just want to be neighborly."

"In that case, it'd be my pleasure to accept your hospitality," McDonald said. His mood lightened, and he pushed out a chair for Slocum.

Slocum poured, then asked, "I need to know something of the watering holes to the north. I intend to reach Santa Fe as quick as I can, but the heat is wearing me down and making my horse puny."

"There are a few holes I know about, one of them on my employers' spread. Don't think they'd mind you using it, as long as you're using it just for your own gullet and your horse's."

"That's all," Slocum said.

"Here's Tularosa and this is Coyote Springs about twelve miles to the north and east," McDonald said, using his finger to draw on the tabletop. He dipped his finger briefly in the whiskey and traced out another portion of map to show Slocum how best to reach the promised watering hole.

"You miserable, horse-thievin' cayuse!" The insult echoed through the saloon and spun both Slocum and McDonald around. Both men's hands went for their six-guns.

Slocum did not relax, but he did not draw either. He didn't know the florid, burly galoot standing there, a scattergun resting in the crook of his arm. If he swung the barrel around, Slocum reckoned he might have to shoot him. A gun like that could kill dozens of people in a room this size—and Slocum knew gunning down George McDonald and himself wasn't much of a chore.

Unless the man behind the shotgun trigger was dancing around, trying to keep his own worthless hide from being ventilated. He might miss with one barrel. Slocum vowed to prevent even this attempt, if it came to that.

"What do you want, Goode? This here saloon's for decent men, not your kind," McDonald said, his words slurring slightly. Slocum was sorry he had bothered to force his liquor on the man now. If McDonald took it into his head to start a war, Slocum would be caught smack in the middle of the gunplay.

Not belonging to either side, he'd get shot at by both sides.

"Your men been stealin' my horses. I got proof of it this time! My foreman saw you out there doin' the thievin'!"

"When, Goode? When am I supposed to have been out there stealing your bony horses?" McDonald showed no anger, but Slocum noticed his fingers tightened a little more around the butt of his six-shooter. McDonald was a dangerous customer and would erupt into action at the smallest sign of trouble.

"This morning, that's when."

"I was here most of the morning. Isn't that right, Monty?" McDonald called to the barkeep. The barkeep had both hands under the bar, reaching for a weapon of some kind. Slocum wondered if it might not be a shotgun to rival the one toted so carelessly by John Goode. If so, Slocum was in danger from three different directions.

"That lyin' bartender would say the sun came up in the west if you tole him to swear to it," Goode grumbled.

"No man calls me a liar, Goode!"

"He's no man, Monty," McDonald said, swinging his long legs out from under the table. He pushed to his feet and squared his stance. He was ready to draw.

"If you think I've been rustlin' your stock, tell it to the sheriff."

"That limp-spined, no account—" Goode started sputtering. Behind him stood a smaller man, hardly coming to Goode's shoulder. But the glint of sunlight off a sheriff's badge told Slocum a fourth gun had been stirred into this deadly stew. The more angry men who joined the fight, the more likely it was that lead would fly. Slocum looked around and decided the back door was his best chance to get to safety. Otherwise, he might have to start shooting men he didn't know and toward whom he bore no malice.

More to the point, during the few minutes he had spoken with George McDonald, he had taken a liking to the man. Slocum wasn't up to shooting it out with a man he might come to call friend.

"Cain't say it's real smart of you to insult a man standin' behind you," the sheriff said. "But then, I never saw much in the way of manners or brains in you, Goode."

"He stole my horses. I got a witness."

"If you mean that fool of a foreman of yours, he didn't see nothin' this morning. He was sleeping off a drunk in the back cell all night. I didn't rouse him till after breakfast. Didn't have to feed the drunkard that way.''

"Billy was in jail? But he said the horses was stolen by—''

"Whatever happened to your horses last night, Billy Franklin didn't see it,'' the sheriff said coldly.

Slocum half rose from his chair just as the back door he had looked to for sanctuary clattered open. Two men stood outlined in the doorway, the bright sun behind them. They had rifles leveled and were ready to start shooting.

"You say the word, Pa, and we'll take care of them.''

"Walter and Charley Goode,'' McDonald muttered under his breath. He stood, hand on his six-shooter and ready for serious fighting. Slocum kicked away his chair and stood also, not sure any of them would survive the cross fire set up by Goode and his sons.

2

"You boys stop it right now!" bellowed the short sheriff. The man foolishly shoved John Goode from his path and stepped forward. The bantam rooster of a lawman might not have shown much horse sense, but his courage was undeniable. The fire shooting from his every glance caused Walter Goode to hesitate.

This gave the barkeep and McDonald time to draw their weapons. McDonald's six-shooter cocked and pointed squarely at John Goode. Monty's sawed-off shotgun aimed at the rear door. A squeeze on the weapon's double triggers would send two barrels of leaden death into Walter and Charley Goode.

For Slocum's part, he considered getting out a window if the need arose. Lead not meant for him flying around presented a hotter environment than out in the noonday sun. He was no coward avoiding a fight, but he was no fool either. This was not a fight anyone would win.

"Your foreman's a liar, Goode," the sheriff said sternly. "Franklin couldn't have seen McDonald or anyone else rustlin' horses."

"But he tole me—"

"Did you even know he was in the hoosegow? He shot up Mangy Ed's saloon, and I tossed him in the lockup to sleep it off."

"He said he was riding fence, Pa," Walter Goode said. The young man considered his chances against Monty's shotgun. Slocum decided Walter would have to be the first to die. Otherwise, the hotheaded youngster was likely to start a battle where more than one would get ventilated.

"We'll have this out with him. He might have lied when he found the horses missing. He was responsible for them," John Goode said.

"Can't be too responsible on the range when he's locked up in town," the sheriff said. "Get on out of Tularosa until you cool off. Though on a day like this, everyone's entitled to be a little hot under the collar. It must be danged near a hundred degrees outside."

Slocum appreciated the way the sheriff deftly shifted from stony defiance in the face of Goode's demands to an easy camaraderie unlikely to spark any trouble.

John Goode motioned to his sons, and they all vanished into the New Mexico heat and dust. The sheriff let out a deep breath and motioned for the bartender to put away his shotgun.

"George," the sheriff said, "You're a lightning rod for trouble. Don't go provokin' them boys again."

"He didn't do anything, Sheriff," Slocum said. "He was helping me out and Goode barged in, making wild accusations."

"Who might you be?" The sheriff's hard eyes worked up and down Slocum's six-foot frame, as if finding such height to be criminal. And to a five-foot-eight man, it might be. Slocum knew he'd have to tread lightly or the sheriff might start flipping through wanted posters. Even in an out-of-the-way place like Tularosa there might be one on him.

"Nobody important, Sheriff," Slocum said. "I'm on my way north to Santa Fe."

"Right now?"

"I'd thought to rest a day."

"There's some mighty nice scrub oak and cottonwoods ten miles north of here. Camping under the stars does a world of good for a body, or so I hear." The sheriff frowned, gave Slocum one last look, and then whirled and left.

"Don't pay Sheriff Earhart no never mind," McDonald said. "He takes his job too serious sometimes. And the heat's making us all a bit on the prickly side."

"Reckon he might be right about camping," Slocum said. "It's been a spell since I stayed in a hotel."

"Don't let him run you off."

"Thank you kindly, but I was only passing through." Slocum took a final shot from the bottle and pushed it toward McDonald. "The rest is yours."

With that, Slocum went to see to provisions and then retrieving his horse. A considerable amount of money vanished from his poke, but Slocum knew the prices were usual, if exorbitant. He strode to the edge of town, ready to mount and ride.

"She fed and curried and watered, mister, but I can't give you back your money," the boy said, seeing Slocum coming up. "Be glad to keep her for another day, but no refunds."

"That's all right," Slocum told the boy. "My plans have a way of changing fast."

"Danged foolish to ride out in the hottest part of the day."

The boy squinted as he peered at the sun dipping down in the west. "You ride into the Mal Pais and this will seem downright freezin' to you. It's *hot* out there."

Slocum nodded. He had been through the badlands before and knew how blistering hot it could be. With luck, he could skirt the worst of the Mal Pais and maybe find that clump of trees Sheriff Earhart had gone on about. Or the water well on the Stuart brothers' spread George McDonald had been willing to let him drink from.

Riding slowly, Slocum was glad to see the last of the buildings that made up Tularosa pass behind him. He had seen the beginning of range wars before, and knew the one between Goode and McDonald was going to catch fire and spread before too much longer. Less than an hour down the road, Slocum blinked from the bright reflection.

He reined in and dismounted, to the sorrel's immense relief.

"What is that in the road?" he wondered aloud. The horse nickered, not caring for anything but the deliverance from Slocum's weight on its back.

The golden glint again dazzled Slocum. He bent and pawed through the dust until he uncovered a partially hidden coin. He picked it up and tossed it from hand to hand for a moment. The metal was almost molten from the hot sun.

"Gold," he said. "My lucky day finding a double eagle." Then he frowned. The coin was too large for a double eagle. This was almost the size of a silver dollar. Holding it up to get a better look at it, he saw curious characters and an eagle on one side. On the other was beaten a symbol he recognized as being an Aztec calendar, the head in the center thrusting out its tongue.

Balancing the coin in his hand, Slocum decided it was at least an ounce of gold. Solid gold, from the way his fingernail cut into the soft rim. He turned it over and over in his hand, then shoved it into a vest pocket for safekeeping.

"Who might have dropped this?" he asked his sorrel. The horse shook her head as if denying all knowledge. Curious, Slocum got off the road and walked along the verge. The road dropped suddenly into an arroyo, long dry since the spring runoffs. The side of the dried wash showed recent passage of a horse.

"Several riders," Slocum decided, studying the spoor more closely. "All heading into the mountains, unless I miss my guess."

He found himself tossed on the horns of a dilemma. Should he continue on his way or pursue the small band of riders who couldn't be more than an hour ahead of him?

Slocum took the gold coin from his pocket, flipped it into the air so it caught the sun every time it turned over, then snared it on the way down. He opened his hand. The Aztec calendar had landed heads-up.

He tucked away the coin and mounted, following the trail. There wasn't anything he had to do in Santa Fe—and the promise of more gold coins was a powerful lure.

The sun sank low on the western horizon as Slocum made his way up the steep slopes leading into the Sacramento Mountains. The trail had been clear most of the day, but he had never caught sight of the men leaving it. He doubted they were much ahead of him, but the rugged terrain cut off direct view for more than a mile or two in most places. The closer he got to the mountains, the shorter the distance he could see ahead.

Even listening hard for the sound of hooves moving across rock did not help Slocum. He had hoped those he pursued might betray themselves in some way. The fever burning in him had grown stronger the more he had thought about the gold coin. Who could afford to lose so much gold?

Only those with more, lots more.

Slocum wondered when the heat would lift. The setting sun seemed to have nothing to do with the crushing inferno, but he knew it took a spell before the rocks cooled and the night winds began blowing. Slocum closed his eyes and let a gust of hot air puffing from the canyon ahead dry the sweat on his face.

He recoiled when a feather blew into his face. Slocum spun and tried to get it away, but it stuck to his sweaty face. He pulled it free and started to throw it away, only to hesitate when he got a good look at it.

"Never seen anything like this," Slocum said to his sorrel. The horse proved indifferent to the bright green feather and its almost liquid quality. Slocum stroked along the quill, letting it ripple under his fingers. He tried to imagine the size of the bird sporting such a long tail feather or wing feather, but couldn't. And the color was unlike anything he'd ever seen in any desert bird's plumage.

Tucking it away inside his shirt for safekeeping, Slocum turned his face to the wind again and took a deep breath. His acute senses caught a sharpness on the wind that betrayed the men he followed. He couldn't be more than a few hundred yards from them.

Slocum tethered his horse, drew his Winchester from the saddle scabbard, then went ahead on foot. He listened hard and kept a sharp eye out for any sign that he was nearing their camp. Even with all his caution, they got the drop on him.

An arrow whizzed past his head and embedded in the dirt ahead of him. Slocum recoiled, not sure what had happened. Then he realized his enemies were behind him, not in front. He swung around, his rifle coming up to target a bronzed body.

Shock kept him from pulling the trigger. He had thought

he had run afoul of a band of Mescalero or even Warm Springs Apache, but no Apache ever decked himself out in such an outrageous getup. A tall-feathered headdress studded with jade and turquoise stole away Slocum's attention. Fancy silver armbands and a leather breechclout provided most of the covering for the warrior's amazingly muscled, bronze body.

Two others jumped from hiding, swinging war clubs studded with skulls of their enemies. No Apache ever carried such a weapon, not when a good knife or stolen rifle worked better.

Slocum fired, but the shot went wild. He found himself grappling with the nearest warrior, his rifle pushed away. Slocum rolled onto his back and got his feet up into the belly of the man trying to bash his brains out with the skull cudgel. A quick tug and Slocum sent the man sailing through the air.

More arrows whizzed past. He rolled to one side in a feint, then quickly went the other, smashing hard into a boulder. He slithered around the big rock like a snake and came to relative safety on the far side, only to find that his rifle still lay in the dirt on the other side of the rock.

"How many of you feathered bastards?" Slocum muttered. He slid his ebony-handled Colt Navy from its holster, knowing he only had five shots. He always rode with the hammer resting on an empty cylinder. He had seen too many men blow holes in their legs accidentally as they rode to take the chance in the hot sun. Now he regretted his caution.

Slocum had five shots and no more. There wouldn't be any chance to reload when this cylinder came up empty. Five shots. Five shots between him and death.

He snapped off a quick shot into the face of a headdress-wearing warrior that sent the man stumbling back, moaning in pain. Slocum knew he hadn't killed him, but the wound ought to keep him out of battle for a while. Crouching low, Slocum waited to make his next shot count. With luck, he might be able to dash around and grab his rifle, giving him another four or five shots.

It wasn't much of a plan, but it beat sitting on his heels and waiting to get skewered.

More arrows clattered against the rock. Slocum grabbed one and looked it over. No Apache had ever fashioned this arrow. No Comanche or Navajo or Ute or Cheyenne had either. Slocum had found an Aztec coin. He now faced Aztec warriors.

He chanced a quick look around the protecting rock, and froze at the sight. Atop a large boulder ten yards away stood a woman so breathtakingly lovely he couldn't put it into words. She wore the same outfit that the warriors did—and she was bare to the waist, as they were. Her jewelry clanked and clattered as she moved like a puff of wind, to disappear behind the rock.

Slocum forced himself to alertness. What was she doing with these Aztec killers? Who was she? And why were they trying to kill him?

He got another glimpse of the woman striding between the rocks, head held high like a princess and trailing a long cape of intricately woven design. A green serpent writhed on the cloth, fashioned from green and gold thread and having twin eyes of the purest red. But the serpent had arms and hands and held in one hand a scepter and in the other a wicked knife.

She turned and looked over her shoulder in his direction. For a moment, their eyes locked, his green with her black. Slocum thought she was mildly amused at his predicament, and he wondered at hers. Then she snapped her fingers and two of the warriors ran up to kneel in front of her. Slocum couldn't hear what was said, but the woman obviously commanded.

Then a third Aztec warrior came up, a tall, well-built man carrying a war lance decorated with white-and-brown feathers. He argued with her while the other two remained kneeling. After a few seconds of contention, she jerked the cape around her shoulders and stalked off without uttering another word.

The man had won the argument. He pointed his lance in Slocum's direction, a clear order to the kneeling warriors to go forth and kill their prey. On impulse, Slocum squeezed off a shot in the Aztec commander's direction. The shot went wide of its mark, but the man still flinched.

This show of human weakness convinced Slocum he wasn't fighting ghosts. The Aztecs had died out years ago. Whoever dressed as those ancient warriors could be frightened—and killed.

A battle cry ripped from the lips of the Aztec chief. Rising from a half-dozen places nearby came other warriors, more than Slocum had realized were hidden in the rocks. He fired and caught one in the belly. The man doubled up and fell, kicking feebly. This was well and good, but Slocum was down to a deuce of shots while facing a half-dozen or more killers.

He caught sight of the woman on a more distant vantage watching the fight. A look of sadness had come to her face, but not a shred of mercy rested there. She might have been angry at losing the argument with the Aztec chief or there might have been more. Slocum wanted to believe she had pleaded his case and had been overruled.

Firing twice more brought down another warrior intent on launching his war lance into Slocum's chest. The Aztec fell heavily, giving Slocum his chance. Using the fallen man's body as a shield, Slocum grabbed the lance and hurled it awkwardly into the center of the cluster of men charging him. The man Slocum had pegged as chief battled the lance away with easy contempt.

"Ai-ai-aiEEE!" came the cry from the chief's lips. The others hefted their weapons and rushed Slocum.

He lunged forward and landed facedown in the dirt, scrambling to reach his rifle. His fingers closed on the Winchester's stock. He drew it toward him even as the warriors thundered up, waving their knives and war clubs and stabbing out with their lances. Slocum prepared to die—but he intended to take at least one more of the Aztec devils with him. His rifle muzzle rose, and he slid his finger across the trigger, then tightened.

The rifle jammed.

3

Slocum fumbled to grab the barrel of the rifle so he could swing it like a club. He wasn't going to let them jab their feather-decorated toad-stickers into him without a fight. They would know they had been in a free-for-all with John Slocum before they finally killed him.

The dull snap of a pistol shot rang out, echoing down the canyon, followed by two more in quick succession. Then it sounded as if the entire battle of Manassas was being refought. Slocum was deafened by the reports from both rifles and pistols that rolled down the rocky canyon and broke over the small battlefield where he fought for his life.

The Aztec warriors froze in their attack, stared at each other for a moment, then turned and fled. For a heart-stopping instant, Slocum thought their chief would regain control and send them back at him. Slocum spun the rifle around and pried loose the round jammed in the receiver. He levered in a new cartridge and lifted the stock to his shoulder, only to see . . .

Nothing.

The Aztecs had vanished into the gathering twilight as surely as if they had been mirages born of the punishing summer sun. Slocum sat in the dust, wondering if he had fallen from his horse, hit his head, and this was all a fever dream conjured from lack of water and too much heat. Then he saw an intricately wrought round silver ornament that had been ripped from one Aztec's armband. Further examination showed the bodies of those he had shot.

"Two," Slocum grumbled. "All I got were two of them." He dropped to one knee and quickly searched the bodies, finding nothing of interest. Wearing only their fancy feathered headdresses and a breechclout left little room for hiding the vast treasure trove of gold he sought.

Neither of the dead men had so much as a speck of gold dust on them in the small pouches dangling at their waists.

Slocum rose, then paused for a moment, something gnawing away at the edge of his mind. He knelt again and studied the feathers in the two warriors' headdresses. He recognized these as eagle feathers and maybe even parrot feathers. Slocum had seen the brightly colored birds when he had made a trip to Mexico City years earlier.

The feathers were nothing like the supremely soft, bright green feather he had found at the mouth of this canyon. He pulled it from inside his shirt and stroked along it. There was a sensual feel to this feather lacking in the others, a softness and texture beyond anything Slocum had ever seen. More than this, the verdant green was unique. He had never come across a color as intense and . . . unnerving.

New bursts of gunfire echoed along the rocky walls, making him wonder if the cavalry had ridden into a nest of the Aztecs and had launched an all-out war.

He stuffed the feather away for safekeeping, stared at the few stars working their way through the black veil of the nighttime sky, and got his bearings. The shots came from the direction of Round Mountain, a spot he knew passing well. But Slocum didn't return to his horse, and he didn't head for Round Mountain. He went after the fleeing Aztecs.

A speck of blood here and a dropped arrow there provided all the trail Slocum needed. Still, the difficulty of his hunt became increasingly apparent as twilight slid into darkness. He wished for a moon, but there wasn't one. The light from the stars gave a dancing, eerie aspect to the terrain. He had explored this country years before—but he might as well have stepped into it for the first time tonight for all he re-membered.

With a decent amount of light, he might have navigated up and down the canyons with some authority. Not now, not tonight, as he hunted down a pack of murderous savages.

Slocum came to a branching canyon. Gunfire still sounded from off to his right.

"Round Mountain," he decided. "Definitely coming from the direction of Round Mountain." But if the warriors weren't caught up in the gunfight, for all their speed in run-ning, who fought so hard? Confusing as the echoes might have been, Slocum reckoned a hundred or more rounds had been fired. He had been in battles during the war where fewer shots were fired.

He snorted in remembrance. There had been more than one battle where green soldiers had gone through the entire fight without once firing. Or if they had used old muskets, as so many had, they had fired their tamping rods or even forgotten to put in the bullets.

That didn't make those fights any less deadly, but who fired as if the fate of the nation depended on it here in the Sacramento Mountains?

Slocum dropped to one knee as he studied the hard ground and rocky expanse around him. Tracking over this terrain was like following a ghost. The warriors didn't have to work particularly hard to cover their tracks. Simply walking on the rock masked their trail.

Dropping down, Slocum pressed his ear to the ground. He heard distant thumps, but could not determine direction. Prowling about, he muttered to himself and found various fresh spoor, none of it giving him the proper path to follow. He finally gave up and sank down, a rocky canyon wall protecting his back so he could think without worrying about attack.

Who was the woman? Her haunting beauty came back to bedevil Slocum. She had authority among the warriors. Two had knelt while she spoke to them, but her power was limited. The chief had come up and taken over quickly, but she had not given in easily. She had argued. Her position was one of power among the warriors, but not complete control.

And her beauty! Slocum got a lump in his throat thinking of it.

"No gold," he said, heaving himself to his feet. "And no Aztecs, not that I can find." He cursed himself for being a poor tracker, even knowing how impossible the task was in the darkness and over such rocky ground. Slocum wasn't sure what he would have done had he overtaken the fleeing Indians, but they had to be the ones who'd dropped the gold coin he still carried in his vest pocket.

He reached up and ran his finger around its outline. Next to the coin rested Robert's watch, his only legacy from his brother after the bitter death during Pickett's Charge.

"So much gold," Slocum mused. Or was it? He had let his greed fire his imagination. A single coin didn't mean there was a mountain of the golden metal waiting to be plundered. But why were Aztec warriors prowling about New

Mexico Territory? And the gold coin was of Aztec origin. He recognized their calendar embossed on the back side of the coin.

A new volley echoed to deafen him. Slocum retraced his path to where the warriors had attacked him. A quick survey of the fight scene told him nothing he didn't already know. It took better than fifteen minutes to find his horse. The sorrel nickered in greeting, ready to calm down after such loud noises had agitated her.

"There, there," Slocum soothed, patting the horse. He dug around in his saddlebags and found a few lumps of sugar to give her. Then he reloaded both his rifle and his six-shooter, this time putting in a full six charges.

The gunfire became sporadic, but it drew Slocum to find out what lay behind it. He had been thwarted trying to learn more about the Aztecs and their beautiful leader—a priestess?—and his curiosity was getting the better of him. Besides, someone might need his help in such a furious gun battle. They might have run afoul of the Aztecs, and any aid he offered might put him back on a golden trail.

Swinging into the saddle, Slocum let his sorrel pick her own way through the tumble of rocks. He barely saw the ground at times, deep shadows masking everything. The only real illumination on the trail came from the increasingly bright band of stars above him, and these provided scant light.

"Whoa, slow, old girl," Slocum cautioned as he reined back and tried to quiet his jittery horse. She tried crow-hopping on him, but Slocum stopped that fast. Getting thrown might mean his death. There was a lull in the shooting, but it had picked up in deadly tempo more times than he could count.

He slid from the saddle and tethered her to a low bush, then advanced on foot as he had before. This time Slocum felt as if every nerve in his body ached from the strain of preventing an ambush.

He had been taken unawares once this night. There wouldn't be a second time.

"We got the son of a bitch, I tell you," came a whispered voice. "There's no way he coulda lived through that last volley!"

"You're full of it, Ivan," came a voice familiar to Slocum. He tried to put a name to it. When he did, a coldness settled in his gut.

Walter Goode.

"Me or Charley caught him in a cross fire. You're not the only one who can use a six-shooter, Walt," came the petulant protest that confirmed Slocum's suspicion.

"He's half Indian and can sneak away whenever he wants. He's done it often enough," Walter Goode said. "We go after him as soon as Pa gets into position."

Slocum made a slow count of the men around him. He guessed Ivan was another of John Goode's sons. Three here and Goode himself in the rocks somewhere upslope. And they had their quarry pinned in the rocks not too far away. Slocum didn't doubt for an instant they had run George McDonald to ground. The venom in Walter Goode's voice said as much. The hatred for their rival's foreman ran deep through the Texas family.

"He's got to be running out of ammo," the one Slocum identified as Ivan said. "If we rush him—"

"He'll drill us. I tell you, he fights like a damned Injun."

"McDonald's no Indian," Walter Goode said. "And Charley's right. We don't know how much ammunition he's got with him. I never figured he'd last this long. He must have fired a hundred rounds already."

"We've got him. I'll rush him and show you!"

"Shut up, Ivan," Walter Goode said. "The only thing that

can come out of rushing him is to get your damn fool head blowed off.''

"McDonald'd have to shoot Ivan somewhere that'd hurt him," snickered Charley Goode. "He ain't got nothin' in his head to damage."

"Quit your bitching," Walter ordered. "Pa's in place about now. What about Uncle Isham?"

Slocum paused. The entire Goode family had gone after George McDonald—and yet the man had survived the deadly trap.

"He's well nigh blind. He's as likely to shoot us as McDonald," Ivan said. "He's to Pa's right. If we're lucky, he won't wing more 'n one or two of us when the shootin' starts up again."

Slocum knew McDonald faced a small army. This accounted for the frantic fusillade that had frightened off the Aztecs. They must have thought every bullet was aimed directly at them. Slocum wondered what shape George McDonald was in after such heavy gunfire. He might have been cut to bloody ribbons.

Knowing this was none of his fight, but still hankering to get a chance to go up against the Goodes, Slocum returned to his tethered horse. It took several minutes of searching to get out all the ammunition for his rifle and six-gun. Burdened with the boxes of ammo, he returned to where Walter, Ivan, and Charley Goode waited for their father's signal to start a new fight.

Slocum could have shot them in the back, but decided it wasn't fair. He never shot animals from ambush, preferring to track them down. These low-down snakes didn't deserve any less than he would give their rattle-tailed brethren. Moving like a shadow, he made his way toward the pile of rocks where George McDonald made his stand.

"You up there?" Slocum called.

"Who's there?" demanded McDonald. "If that's you, Goode, I—"

"It's me, Slocum. You showed me the trail to Santa Fe this morning in the saloon in Tularosa."

"I must have done a danged poor job of it. This is nowhere near the road to Santa Fe."

"Took a small furlough from traveling," Slocum said, sliding forward. "How you fixed for ammunition?"

He felt rather than saw George McDonald tense, thinking this was some trap set by the Goodes.

"I've got two boxes for my Winchester," Slocum said, "and enough powder, caps, and ammo for my Colt Navy to fight the rest of the night. What you using?"

"The rifle ammo's fine if you're shooting .45s."

"Here," Slocum said, sliding a box forward into the darkness. A pale hand reached out, closed on the box, and pulled it back. It took McDonald a few seconds to be sure the ammo wasn't bait in a trap. Slocum followed the box over the top of the rock and settled beside the man.

"You still in one piece?"

"One piece," McDonald acknowledged, "but ventilated. They hit me a couple times." From what he could tell, Slocum thought McDonald was a liar. No fewer than ten wounds showed up, none serious, but still slowly leaking the man's lifeblood. McDonald wouldn't be strong enough to put up much of a fight by sunrise unless he got patched by a doctor.

"They're planning a frontal attack," Slocum said. "I overheard Walter and somebody named Ivan talking."

"Ivan's the idiot son, not that Walter or Charley are mental giants," McDonald said. He filled the magazine of his rifle and put a handful of cartridges into his pocket to be able to reach them easily.

"There's an uncle out there too, along with John Goode."

"That'd be the lot of them, I reckon." McDonald heaved

a sigh. "Thanks, Slocum. You didn't have to do this."

Grating of leather across rock alerted Slocum. He swung up and fired almost point-blank into the man coming across a rocky field. Whoever it was went down, screeching like a scalded dog.

"Didn't kill him, but he's winged," Slocum said. And then he found himself shot at from all sides. Slocum settled into the coldly efficient killing machine that he had been during the war. He fired, he reloaded, he found new targets, and then there were no more.

"Think we drove 'em off, Slocum," McDonald said in a weak voice.

Slocum checked. He had gone through an entire box of ammo. He reloaded from the few cartridges in the box he had given McDonald, and only then did he see how bad a shape the man was in.

"You've been hit a dozen times," Slocum said. "I'm getting you into Tularosa."

"Won't argue about it," McDonald said. He slumped, unconscious.

It took Slocum almost an hour to fetch his sorrel, then find McDonald's mount tethered a mile off. Here and there he found evidence that the Goodes had fled. Slocum never doubted McDonald would have died if he hadn't come to his rescue, but he knew it would be nip and tuck whether the man lived until they reached Tularosa.

Three hours later, he rode slowly into town, McDonald draped over his horse's back. What passed for nightlife in town was in full swing, but the sheriff came out, as if sniffing the spilled blood.

"What you been up to, mister?" the banty rooster of a man demanded.

"The Goodes bushwhacked McDonald. I helped him out, but he's past anything I can do."

"Dead?"

"Might be, but he was still bleeding a mile down the road. A doctor might patch him up."

"Somebody sober up Doc Benoit and get him to his office. Get George up there and ready for the doc," Sheriff Earhart ordered. He stared up at Slocum, pursed his lips, then said, "Get on down, and I'll buy you a drink."

"Name's Slocum." Slipping from the saddle, Slocum decided there wasn't much way he could avoid having the lawman notice him. Being straight was a good way to deflect any suspicion.

They went into a bar with a sign so faded Slocum couldn't read it. The saloon was nothing more than a wood plank balanced between two sawhorses. This wasn't the finest drinking emporium in Tularosa, but it served better whiskey than the other place Slocum had gone.

"The Goodes did this?" Earhart asked, knocking back his drink. He slammed the shot glass to the plank bar.

"Saw Walter, Ivan, and Charley," Slocum said. "They talked about an uncle and their pa."

Earhart's gaze dropped to the butt of Slocum's Colt in its cross-draw holster. Slocum knew what went through the man's mind. The ebony handle showed long use.

"I'm no gunslinger," Slocum said. "I'm just on my way to Santa Fe."

"Then get on the road right now," Earhart said sharply. "I don't need hired gunmen adding to the trouble brewin' around here. I wish to high heaven John Goode had never come to Tularosa. Damn him, damn every cowpuncher in Texas."

Boot heels clicking on the rotting wood floorboards, the sheriff spun and stalked off.

Slocum wasn't inclined to argue with the lawman.

4

"Don't reckon you want another," the barkeep said, too fast to be civil. He rubbed his dirty hands on the front of an even dirtier shirt. His handlebar mustache twitched slightly at the frayed ends, betraying a growing nervousness.

"One more," Slocum said. The barkeep didn't move. "There a problem with me having another drink?"

"Sheriff Earhart wanted you out of Tularosa." The twitchy man's eyes darted to the six-shooter holstered at Slocum's hip.

"I'm not going to kill anybody, not at this time of night." Slocum pulled out the pocket watch and flipped open the worn case. It was almost dawn. He had been through Hell and hadn't gotten a wink of sleep, yet he felt as fresh as if he'd just beaten the rooster onto the fence to outcrow him.

"There's talk around town," the bartender said, his nervousness growing. "Range war. Nobody likes the notion."

"Figure I'd hire out?"

The barkeep nodded vigorously, his mustache trembling. His face turned a shade paler under the grime, and he tossed aside a bar rag he had been twisting into a knot.

"Who'd pay my price in this one-horse town?" Slocum reached past the man and grabbed the bottle of whiskey, pouring his own shot. He was getting tired of this byplay and wanted to be on his way, yet a perverse streak made him badger the barkeep.

"The Goodes don't need you. They got too much family already," the barkeep said, backing off. Slocum saw the butt of a six-shooter under the plank serving as a bar, and knew the man was being backed into a corner. Even a rat could fight.

"You figure the Stuarts would hire me because I brought back their foreman?"

The barkeep nodded and sidled closer to the gun. Slocum shrugged, finished his drink, dropped a silver dollar on the plank with a bright ring, and then walked out. He had had enough of Tularosa and the petty feuds brewing here. It all meant nothing. He had been in the midst of too many battles over grazing rights, water, and even whether to grow cattle or wheat. It all turned boring after a spell—deadly nonetheless, but also unending and boring.

He had no stake in Tularosa. The liquor here was watered, and the storekeepers charged too much for essential supplies. The women were all ugly or taken, and he had no reason to stay. He wished George McDonald well and hoped the Goodes got their comeuppance, but Slocum's heart wasn't in it. Not the way it was in finding out what really went on up the Sacramento Mountains with the Aztecs and their beautiful half-naked priestess.

As Slocum swung into the saddle, her memory returned to haunt him. Why was she here? Why were the Aztec warriors here? Gold, maybe. But something more was going on with the feathered Indians. They had come a long way—for what? Only gold?

Slocum knew his curiosity got him into a powerful load of trouble at times, and this was likely to be one of those times. Still, he wondered why the warriors had jumped him, and where they had gotten off to so fast when the gunfire spooked them like edgy rabbits with a coyote sniffing their tails.

Snorting, he turned his sorrel northward again, and rode till almost dawn before coming to a decision. The Aztecs were a puzzle to solve. Slocum smiled wryly when he realized he'd like to catch sight of their priestess again too. There was a magnetic quality to her beauty that pulled Slocum's compass needle away from Santa Fe and to the mountains.

By noon he had located the spot where the Aztecs had attacked him the night before. It didn't surprise him that the two bodies were gone. He dropped to the rocky ground and worked to find where the corpses had been dragged. It proved harder than he thought. The Aztecs were good at covering their trail.

Slocum was better at finding it. By late afternoon he had located their trail and was slowly making his way up a canyon with steep sides that turned him increasingly uneasy. A sentry on either rim could spot him in a flash. He drifted toward one canyon wall. He was easier to spot from the far rim, but almost impossible to see from above. Slocum realized he had improved his chances by half without knowing he had done it.

With the rocky wall at his left, he went deeper into the canyon. He didn't need to follow the Aztecs' trail. There was nowhere for them to go, unless they turned into birds and flew away. He saw a spot where it might lead to a path up the face of the cliff, but Slocum doubted they were going up. Something about this narrow canyon held them, just as figuring out what the Aztecs were up to kept Slocum doggedly on their trail.

It didn't take long before shadows began dropping across the canyon as the sun dipped behind the steep walls. Slocum considered taking a rest. He had been on the go almost a full day. Taking only a few minutes to eat some jerky along the way, he found he was more tired than he was hungry at the moment.

"Time to rest," Slocum said. "No telling how far this canyon winds." He patted the sorrel, dismounted, and let the horse crop away at a juicy patch of blue grama. He pulled some sourdough bread and more of the tough jerky from his saddlebags, thought for a moment, then dredged up a can of peaches. Slocum wasn't that hungry, but he didn't know when he would get a chance to eat again.

Settling down, he gnawed at the stale bread and tore off a chunk of the salted meat. He chewed hard for a few minutes, then stopped and cocked his head to one side. Slocum's eyes widened when he realized how close he had come to finding the Aztecs—to actually riding over them. The sounds rose and then fell to nothing.

"Digging sounds?" Slocum wondered aloud. He swallowed the rest of his meal without tasting it, which might have been a good thing, then put the can of peaches back into his saddlebags. The horse shied as he reached for the reins. The horse was as tired as he was, but he had to move on now.

"A few more miles," Slocum urged. He swung into the saddle and walked the horse through the gathering gloom. Not two hundred yards ahead, Slocum saw the golden glow of torches. A huge bonfire had been lit in the center of the ring of torches, but the area around it seemed deserted.

Thinking the torches might be markers for the Aztec sentries, Slocum dismounted and approached one guttering torch as silently as possible. To his surprise the torch had been thrust between two rocks to keep it upright, but no warrior waited near it.

A slow circuit of the camp took almost twenty minutes. All Slocum found were the torches at what he considered the perimeter of the Aztec camp. Of the Indians he saw nothing. As he started into the camp to study the area closer to the bonfire, he heard the clanking and scrape of metal against rock.

Turning from the campsite, he studied the canyon walls. It took him almost ten minutes to find the dark hole that showed where a mine shaft sank into the side of the mountain.

He had been prowling too long and had paid little attention to his back after discovering no Indians around. This almost cost him his life.

From behind came the whoosh of an Aztec war club. Slocum's hand went toward his six-gun as he dropped into a gunfighter's crouch, ready to whirl around. Only this instinctive move saved him. The war club crashed into his shoulder.

Pain shot through his body and turned his right arm numb. His fingers fought vainly to close around the butt of his Colt Navy. Slocum tried to grab at the gun with his left hand, but had no chance. The warrior swarmed forward and tried to bash his brains out again.

Slocum hit the ground hard and got his knees up in time to force the Aztec away. The club crashed into the ground beside Slocum's head, but he wasn't staying put. He kicked and tangled his legs in the warrior's. The two of them grappled on the ground, rolling over and over.

He kept trying to get a hold on the Aztec, but his right arm refused to work. And with the Indian swarming constantly, swinging the club awkwardly, forcing him to avoid the bone-crushing blows, Slocum wasn't able to get his six-shooter free.

Flailing around, Slocum swung his right arm out like a dead tree limb to smash into the side of the warrior's head. This produced the first outcry—and Slocum knew he was doomed.

The cry would alert the others toiling in the depths of the mine.

He redoubled his efforts, to no avail. The Aztec smashed a bony fist into his chest and knocked him flat. Gasping for breath, Slocum watched the Indian raise his club. Then the warrior simply froze like a statue.

With vision dipped in molasses, Slocum watched the Aztec sink to the ground. He couldn't figure out what had happened. He fumbled at his left side and found the six-gun still in its holster. He somehow hadn't drawn and fired. He couldn't decide what had happened until he heard the urgent voice that pulled him out of his curious state.

"You are not harmed. Please, come with me or they *will* kill you!"

Blinking hard and wiping the sweat from his eyes, Slocum saw the Aztec priestess. She was lovelier than ever—and still bare to the waist. But her feminine attributes weren't what held his gaze. The bloody knife in her hand showed why the warrior had simply stopped fighting.

He had died with her knife in his back.

"Why'd you save me?" Slocum asked, getting to his feet. He rubbed his numb arm, wondering if something had been broken.

"Come, hurry. You cannot stay here any longer. Pitalpitoque soon will learn his guard is gone."

"What?" Slocum tried to figure out what she had said. He winced when she grabbed him by the arm and insistently pulled. The daze from being struck faded, and Slocum pulled free of her grip.

"He will never let you live," she said. "He will come after you, and there is no way for you to stop him."

"Him? This Pit—whatever?"

"He is a monster, and I can no longer control him."

"Are you a priestess of some kind?" Slocum saw the intricate silver conches filled with Aztec designs that decorated her belt and armbands. The work that had gone into her jewelry indicated something far more than a simple Mexican *peon*.

"I worship Quetzalcoatl, the feathered serpent," she said. "I saw you before. You fight well, but this is not your battle. Go, run far away from here."

"Seems purty near everyone's telling me that," Slocum said. He started to ask about the gold coin he had found, then changed his mind. She was upset and seemed genuinely concerned about his welfare. "Why do you care?"

"Things have gotten out of hand," she said.

"My name's John Slocum."

"You must flee. You meddle in things beyond your understanding!"

"Pleased to meet you," Slocum went on. "I didn't catch your name."

"Angelina," she said brusquely. "I am from Lake Texcoco near Tenochtitlán and am of Aztec descent."

"Guessed as much," Slocum said. He pulled out the green feather and held it in front of him. "What do you make of this, Angelina?"

Her dark eyes went wide. She reached for the feather, then pulled back as if it burned her fingers.

"How did you come by this? No! Do not tell me!" She looked at him, a difference in her eyes now. She had been anxious before. Now Slocum found it difficult to put a word to the emotions playing across her face and deep into her dark eyes.

"What's going on?" Slocum asked. Angelina seemed tossed on the horns of a dilemma. Slocum saw decision harden on her face. She took his arm again and guided him away from the bonfire and toward the far canyon wall.

"We will be safer here. We can talk, but only for a few minutes," she said. With the grace of a deer, Angelina made her way through the darkness. Now and then Slocum caught sight of a bare breast, a curving hip, the silhouette of a beguiling woman. He had come after the Aztecs hunting for gold.

Or was that all? He had seen her before. Was he going to get his head blown off because he was thinking with his cock? Greed was one thing, getting involved with a woman as mysterious as Angelina was something entirely different—and infinitely more deadly.

"Are you in charge? I saw how they knelt in front of you and—"

"I am priestess, but he is Pitalpitoque. He carries the spirit of a great war chief in his breast. There is a conflict now, and I fear he is turning greedy."

"What are you hunting? The gold?" Her eyes widened in shock as he said this.

"You have the feather. You are chosen, so of course you would know all this," Angelina said, making Slocum even more curious about what was going on.

"How many of them are there?" Slocum asked, pointing back in the direction of the mine shaft.

"You must not fight Pitalpitoque. He is a great warrior and has the spirit of Montezuma's greatest general hidden inside his breast."

"Unless he's a ghost, there's no reason a slug in the gut won't stop him. But what would I gain if I did that?"

"You are chosen," she said again, moving closer. "I never have found one who was. Not before."

"Chosen for what?" asked Slocum. And then he found concentrating more difficult. Her bare breasts rubbed against his chest. Arms circling him, Angelina pulled him closer. As much as Slocum wanted answers, he found himself willing to be diverted for a time.

He returned the kiss and began working away from her full lips, down the sweep of her throat, to those luscious, firm, naked breasts. His mouth closed over one nipple and worked the nub he found under his tongue until it turned rubbery and pulsed with every beat of her heart.

"You are chosen," Angelina said enigmatically. Her fingers stroked all over his body, touching here and gliding there, arousing him with every contact of her strong brown fingers.

"I'm glad you chose me," Slocum said, still not sure what she meant by that. Then he stopped talking and went back to using his mouth all over the glorious surge of her breasts. He moved lower and unfastened the leather strap around her waist. The dark triangle between her bronzed legs drew him powerfully.

He reached out and stroked over the mound, bringing moans of delight to her lips.

"How can I give you pleasure?" she asked. Together they sank to the ground. Slocum shucked off his shirt and pants, using them as a crude blanket. Angelina lay back and opened herself willingly to him. He dropped between her thighs and moved forward, his manhood aching with need. With a single move, he slid forward and deep into her trembly interior.

She gasped and lifted her legs even higher, locking her ankles behind his back, as if to keep him from escaping. The way Slocum felt, surrounded by her tight sheath of female flesh, he would never leave.

They lay locked together for several minutes, hips unmoving, their mouths saying it all with wet kisses and gentle
swipes along sensitive flesh. But Slocum eventually felt pres-
sures mounting within him that forced him to begin moving.

He withdrew slightly, his thickness still parting her nether
lips. He gazed down at her and saw the expression on her
face. Passion, yes. Lust, definitely. But there was more, and
it worried him. But not enough to take away from the urgency that had mounted within his loins. He stroked forward,
then pulled away, falling into the ages-old rhythm of a man
loving a woman.

She began moaning louder and writhing under him. This
spurred him on. His excitement matched hers, and soon he
was trying to split her in half with his fleshy sword. Angelina
arched her back and ground her hips in a circular motion
every time he vanished completely into her interior. Her female flesh clutched down hard all around him and told him
he was close, very close.

"Can't keep going much longer. Feel like a young buck
with his first woman," he said. "You're so pretty."

"You are chosen," Angelina grated out. Then she gasped
and a ripple of intense pleasure flooded her. The wave caught
Slocum and crushed down on his hidden length. The white
tide exploded from deep within his balls and blasted forth as
Angelina's fingers clawed at his back. She thrashed about,
and the two of them strove together until the intense grip of
passion faded.

They lay side by side, arms circling each other. Slocum
wasn't quite sure what to say. From the first brief glimpse
of Angelina, he had wondered what it would be like to make
love to her, but he had never thought it would happen—and
not so quick. It was a lightning bolt in the night. Blinding,
dazzlingly beautiful, undeniably intense, and over in a flash.

What now? He had no idea.

5

"You are something of a mystery," Slocum finally said. "Why are you here? It's a long way from Mexico City, from Tenochtitlán." The word didn't roll easily off his tongue and he didn't much care. It wasn't that he thought Angelina was lying, but the story she spun was a pretty tall tale.

"We hunt that which is our legacy," Angelina said, saying less than Slocum wanted to hear. His thoughts turned to the pure gold coin resting in his vest pocket, the warriors busy digging away in their mine, the way he had been attacked—and Pitalpitoque.

Slocum smiled wryly. Gold was a powerful goad. With the man who thought he was possessed by an ancient ghost, Slocum shared that avarice.

"What will you do with it if you get it?" he asked.

Angelina sat up. In the dim light he saw shadows moving across her naked beauty, and felt stirrings again. Never had he found a woman so lovely or so enigmatic. She had saved him, but only when he had shown her the green feather had her attitude toward him changed. For the better, Slocum allowed, but definitely Angelina had changed the way she looked at him.

"It must be returned to the people of Montezuma. When Cortés fought Montezuma II, great wealth was taken away and hidden in the land where Montezuma's father had been born."

"Here? Montezuma's pa was born here?"

"He was. Near where you call Fort Sumner. Montezuma II felt confident the Spanish would never reach this far north." She snorted in contempt. "They did, of course, but they never found the gold."

"There's a mountain of gold around here?" Slocum asked, his heart beating faster. A single coin *had* been a clue to a treasure trove. One coin of how many? He literally sought to unearth a king's ransom, even if the king was of a long-dead people.

"We know it is here, but where is a problem. The instructions left by Pitalpitoque are vague."

"Wait, hold on. Pitalpitoque? If he knows—"

"Not *this* Pitalpitoque, the one who fought Cortés. The chief leading his warriors in the hunt for the gold now is possessed by the spirit of Pitalpitoque."

"Seems he ought to be able to just ask this ghost hiding away inside where he buried the gold three hundred years ago."

"I will not allow that," Angelina said. Slocum shook his head. He didn't cotton much to this religious mumbo jumbo. "I control the spirit of the Pitalpitoque who has gone before, and will not let him speak directly."

"So this Pitalpitoque needs you?"

"Yes," she said. "And I am not sure I want this Pitalpitoque to find the treasure. I fear he is more possessed by greed than duty, and will keep the gold for himself rather than returning it to Tenochtitlán, where it belongs to everyone.''

''Don't know that much of history, but I seem to remember Montezuma wasn't too big on sharing with his treasure.''

''The gold is the legacy of the Aztec people,'' Angelina said firmly. Slocum finished dressing. Angelina got into her clothing in far less time due to its skimpiness. She stood and moved about restlessly in the darkness, starlight flashing off the silver ornaments at her arms and waist.

''How good a general was Pitalpitoque—way back when?'' asked Slocum, not sure what to say.

''Good, very good. He held Cortés at bay for weeks against the Spaniard's fire sticks.''

''Muskets,'' Slocum said.

''That is so,'' Angelina said. ''This man now who calls himself Pitalpitoque is not half as clever or able to command.''

''He still has the upper hand,'' Slocum said, discounting Angelina's power over the man. As long as Pitalpitoque thought Angelina was useful, he would keep her around. If she persisted in opposing him, she would be killed and left in some arroyo for the buzzards.

''I will cut him off from his information,'' she said.

''You can't do it without him killing you,'' Slocum said. He saw this did not matter to the woman. She was a priestess of Quetzalcoatl and thought this status protected her from any evil. He wondered how to convince her she was wrong.

''I need your help, John Slocum. Let Pitalpitoque find the gold, but then we must see that it is returned to Tenochtitlán where it belongs. You are chosen to aid in this. I have seen the sign left you by Quetzalcoatl. You are chosen.''

''Don't know much about politics down Mexico way, but

things were a bit corrupt last I heard. The government would never let you give away gold to *peones*."

"They cannot stop me. Quetzalcoatl is my protector."

Slocum shook his head. He had run into religious zealots before, but usually with a god more familiar.

"Where is this Quetzalcoatl? Can you trot him out to help us right now? If you can, we will take care of Pitalpitoque and be done with a whale of a lot of trouble."

"He is the feathered serpent god, not my servant. I obey his will, not the other way around. Where he is and what he does at the moment are not mine to question."

"Then it's up to us," Slocum said. He felt a mite guilty about going even this far. He wanted the gold Angelina sought, and considered it his due for all he had been through. The Aztecs had tried to kill him twice, and twice warriors had ended up dead. It wouldn't take much more of that before Pitalpitoque got downright angry and decided to stop looking for the gold and started shooting at Slocum full-time.

If only Angelina wasn't so adamant about returning the gold to her people. A split might be worked out that would be acceptable to both of them. Slocum knew a hundred places where he could spend a stack of gold coins on a woman as lovely as Angelina.

"Quetzalcoatl wills it," she said. "He protects the treasure of the Aztecs, and I must obey his commands."

Slocum settled the six-shooter in its cross-draw holster and then asked, "How many men with Pitalpitoque?" The name tangled his tongue, but Angelina had no trouble with it.

"Pitalpitoque commands a dozen men. Rather, there are twelve left. We lost two on the way here, and you have killed two."

"And you finished off a fifth one. That's going to make

the surviving fighters a mite edgy. They're getting close to losing half their number.''

''You will do this for me?'' She moved closer, and Slocum's resolve faded. He had decided to back off and let the crazy chief who thought he was possessed by a ghost find the gold, then steal it from him. But somehow, the woman had managed to cloud his judgment—with greed and her undeniable charms.

''What do you want me to do?''

''We must stop him from keeping the gold after he finds it. The curse on it will destroy him if he does not bow to Quetzalcoatl's will.''

''Curse? Quetzalcoatl's curse?'' Slocum didn't know whether to laugh or spit in disgust.

''No one can seize the gold for his own. It is the Aztec people's legacy. The feathered serpent will see that it is given only to its rightful owners.''

''All right,'' he said, waiting to cross that bridge later when they found the gold. ''What—?''

Gunfire interrupted him. He cocked his head to one side, knowing he listened to echoes coming from back down the canyon. The Aztecs used lances and bows and arrows, not rifles. Moreover, they were up-canyon from where he and Angelina had made love. The last time he had checked on such gunfire he had found George McDonald pinned down by Goode and his family. What he might find this time was a real puzzle.

''Who fights?'' Angelina asked.

''There's one way of finding out. The shots won't stop Pitalpitoque if he thinks he is on to the gold, but we don't want anyone blundering in and mucking up his hunt.'' Slocum knew there were enough armed Goodes to take away any size treasure from the poorly armed Aztecs. Not for an instant did he believe John Goode and his boys wouldn't steal a pile of gold if they came upon it, rightful owner or Quetzalcoatl's curse notwithstanding.

"Do you think someone hunts game?" she asked.

So far there had been few shots. Three? Slocum thought he'd heard that many, possibly a fourth. And that was all. He doubted any hunter worth his salt would fire that many times at a deer. But one man shooting at another was a different matter.

"Two-legged game is my guess," Slocum said. "Come on. We'll settle that matter, then get back and find out if Pitalpitoque has uncovered your gold yet."

Slocum took off, making his way through the darkness, heading back down the canyon to where his horse waited nervously. The sorrel had been frightened too many times. It took several minutes for Slocum to gentle her. And when he mounted, he noticed that Angelina had vanished. Either she had not kept up with him, or had chosen to follow a different path. He shrugged it off. From the way she talked about her feathered god, she thought it was Slocum's destiny to help return the gold to Tenochtitlán in the middle of Lake Texcoco.

He wheeled his sorrel about and cantered down the rocky trail out of the canyon, finding a branching trail that seemed about right. Another half mile of riding brought him to a point where he heard loud cries and muttered curses. He swung from the saddle and approached on foot, wary of an ambush. Walter Goode looked to be the kind of owlhoot willing to put a bullet in a man's back just for the fun it afforded.

Slocum drew his six-shooter and went exploring. He found a horse wandering loose, its reins dragging. A bit farther up the steep trail leading to the rim he saw movement, shadow within shadow. Glancing back down the slope, he found a small line shack, hardly big enough to walk into and back out of. Another horse was tethered outside.

Walking as if his boots had turned to eggshells, Slocum edged up the small, rocky trail until he came within a dozen feet of the two men. One cradled the other's head and, from the way he cried, had been the source of the loud cries Slocum had heard earlier.

"What's going on?" he asked, cautiously glancing over his shoulder just to be sure.

"They butchered him. They cut him down!" sobbed the man. "He was a friend, a good friend."

"Who is it?" Slocum moved closer and saw the dead man's face. He went cold inside. "I left him back in Tularosa to be patched up by the doctor. What's McDonald doing out here?"

"His job, dammit!" The man flared. "He wasn't going to lollygag in town when there was work to do. George came out to the shack and they murdered him, the back-shooting bastards!"

"The Goodes?"

"Who else could it be?" The man turned an angry face toward Slocum, as if suddenly considering him a potential threat. His hand went toward the six-gun holstered at his side. He stopped when he saw Slocum's hand rise and the Colt Navy aim directly for his head.

"Don't do anything foolish. I saved him from the Goodes. I'm not his enemy."

"You're Slocum. I heard the sheriff talking about you. My name's Lee, Oliver Lee."

"Can't say I'm pleased to meet you considering the circumstances. How long back do you think McDonald got bushwhacked?" Slocum saw the dead man hadn't worn a side arm. Considering all that had happened to McDonald, this was a damn fool oversight and one that had spelled his death.

"I heard the shots as I was riding up. I think I heard a horse galloping off, but I didn't see anyone."

"You came up from town?"

"From that way," Lee said, gesturing toward the line shack. "Tularosa isn't more than ten miles off."

"Do tell." Slocum spat in disgust. He had been wandering around in the mountains and had gotten turned around. Town was only a couple hours ride off, and he had managed to turn it into an all-day ride.

"I heard three shots, maybe four," Slocum said. Oliver Lee nodded in agreement. Slocum knelt and studied George McDonald's body. Not only had he been unarmed, his killer had shot him down from the back. McDonald had never even seen his killer, of if he had, he had been running away.

Either way, the man who had shot McDonald had cut him down in cold blood.

"Which way was he laying when you found him?"

"I think he was hiking to the top of the rim. From up there at sunrise you can get a good view of most of the Stuart spread. He had a pair of binoculars." Oliver Lee pointed to a shattered pair some distance away.

"Think he even knew anyone was here?"

Lee shook his head and wiped tears from his eyes. "He was going to marry my niece, Nettie. He was like family— and he was going to *be* family."

Range war. Slocum remembered how spooked the barkeep had been, and how adamant the sheriff had been about running out of Tularosa anyone who might take part in such a war. The way Lee talked, it was turning into a blood feud, the only thing that might be worse than a range war. No amount of killing ever satisfied the family of a man brutally murdered.

Even the sight of the entire Goode family with nooses around their necks wouldn't be enough, Slocum knew.

He stood and prowled around the area. He found where a man—possibly two—had crouched behind a greasewood waiting for McDonald. No shells were to be found; Slocum thought the shots he had heard had come from a six-gun. The heavier pop of a rifle had been missing in this deadly barrage.

"Four shots, from ambush," he muttered. He wandered upslope and found a spot where two horses had been tethered, confirming his suspicion about the number of attackers. Frowning, he dropped to his knees and ran his fingers along the ground. They came up wet and sticky.

"What you find, Slocum?"

Slocum jerked around, hand going to his six-shooter. He stopped when he saw Sheriff Earhart. The short lawman bustled over, thumbs hooked into his gunbelt.

"Can't say. Since McDonald didn't have a gun, I'd say one of the horses stepped on a Spanish bayonet."

Earhart dropped to the ground and peered along it. He took a few minutes to survey the rocky expanse, and then crept along. Slocum watched, wondering if the sheriff knew what he was doing. When he found the sharp-spined plant Slocum had guessed at, Slocum knew the man was a pretty good tracker.

"Broke off one of the spines," Earhart said, touching the knee-high plant. He ran his finger down the side of the knife-blade-sized spine. "Blood accumulated. See how the horse stomped around? Must have gone deep into its leg."

"If the horse is limping, the rider won't get far before pulling up lame. Do you think the second rider will stick with his partner?"

"Second rider?"

Slocum smiled slightly. He had seen what the lawman

hadn't. Maybe Sheriff Earhart wasn't such a good tracker after all. For some reason, that made Slocum feel a mite better.

That and the anger burning darkly on the short man's face.

6

Slocum peered into the darkness, trying to catch any glimpse of Angelina. She had left him back in the canyon where Pitalpitoque and his Aztecs worked so diligently to uncover their golden treasure. He had the eerie feeling of being watched, and hoped it was the lovely priestess. If Pitalpitoque was spying on him, Slocum could expect only a feathered arrow in the back.

"What do you see out there in the night, Slocum?" asked Sheriff Earhart. "It wouldn't be the varmints who killed McDonald. They wouldn't stay around, not after such a vile act."

"All four shots in the back?" Slocum asked, turning from his study of the darkness down the canyon. He was torn between returning to find Angelina and pursuing the men who had cut down George McDonald. He had no stake in finding the foreman's killers, but gunning a man down from

51

ambush—and shooting him in the back—worried at Slocum like a burr under the saddle blanket.

"Nope," said Earhart. He took out a plug of tobacco, bit off a plug, and started to chew. Only after he spat did he continue. "Best I can tell, only three shots hit him."

"I heard four," Slocum said, remembering the gunshots. He might have confused the echoes down the steep-walled canyons, but he didn't think so.

"So they missed with one round," the sheriff said. "It hardly matters."

"It does," Oliver Lee called out. "Lookee what I found." The man came up, his bowed legs showing considerable space between them. This was a man who had spent most of his life astride a horse.

"A smear of lead?" asked Earhart, taking a large rock and turning it over and over in his hands. "No, you're right, Ollie, this is without a doubt a bullet."

"From the killer's gun? Be hard to prove," Slocum said.

"Gives me a hint who done it," Lee said. "There's not much here, but it is intact." Taking out a large-bladed knife, he pried out the slug from where it had wedged in the crack in the rock. He held it up for Slocum and Earhart to examine.

"Small caliber," Slocum observed. "Couldn't be more than a .32, 'less most of the slug was split off." He took the slug and saw it was deformed but otherwise whole. The round had come from a small-bore six-shooter.

"There's not too many in these parts using a gun that size," Sheriff Earhart said. "Walter Goode is one of them. And he's a dead-on shot with that toy six-shooter of his."

"Anyone else?" Slocum asked.

"Can't think of anyone. What's the size of that six-gun at your hip, Slocum?" asked Earhart.

"It's a .36," Slocum said slowly, wondering what he was getting involved in.

"You surely did get on the scene fast. Ollie here says you came riding up hell-bent for leather, and your gun's been used hard lately."

Slocum said nothing. To tell the sheriff about the Aztecs would put Angelina in jeopardy—and erase any chance he had of getting a share of the hidden gold Pitalpitoque and his warriors sought in the mine.

"What's the reason for him to cut down George?" asked Oliver Lee. "He's just passing through."

"I'm afeared of a range war, Ollie. You know that. Might be that Goode hired Slocum to do some dirty work, thinking we'd ignore the fact he just blew into town."

"You accusin' me, Sheriff?" Slocum considered what he could do. There was no doubt in his head he could outdraw Earhart. He could outdraw both the sheriff and Oliver Lee. But if he did, he would be branded a triple killer. One death might be ignored, but the Stuart brothers could never push aside three deaths.

A posse would dog his tracks all the way into Mexico.

The thought of Mexico revived his greed for Aztec gold— and Angelina.

"Sorry you think that, Sheriff. Here," Slocum said, reaching down and carefully pulling his Colt Navy from its holster. "You want to toss me in the hoosegow, I won't put up a fight. I'm innocent of this killing. I hardly knew McDonald, but I don't know the Goodes at all."

"He rescued George from them back-shooters before, Sheriff," said Lee. "It's no good tossing him in jail when we need all the help we can muster. We got a fight on our hands. If Slocum's willing to join us, let him."

"I wasn't accusing you, Slocum," Earhart said slowly. "It's just a coincidence you happened through Tularosa when all this shootin' and killin' started."

"That's right, Sheriff. Just a coincidence."

"Keep your damn gun. You willing to help us get George's body back to town?"

"Reckon so," Slocum said, wishing he could simply leave. He felt as if he'd thrust his head into a noose and the rope was beginning to chafe a mite. When it tightened, he would be doomed, yet he had no real choice. If he didn't join the lawman and the posse sure to form to go after Walter Goode and the second rider with him, Slocum knew how the Stuarts and those on their side in this skirmish would react.

The trapdoor would open under his feet.

Slocum and Oliver Lee hoisted the corpse and lugged it downhill to the line shack. For the second time, Slocum slung McDonald over the saddle. This time no drunk small-town doctor would be able to patch up the man. As they rode slowly back to Tularosa in silence, Slocum thought hard. He hadn't come up with any alternative to joining the posse that also let him go after the gold hidden away in the mountains.

"There you are, Sheriff!" came the call from a man in Tularosa. Slocum saw a battered star shining on the man's vest. A deputy. "We got a man missing."

"Who's off on a toot now?" Earhart asked tiredly. "I got a murder on my hands, Jed."

Jed looked from Slocum to Oliver Lee and then to his sheriff. "It ain't like that. Perry Altman is the one who's turned up gone."

"So?"

"His wife reported it. She ain't seen him in hours and hours, and he was supposed to be home. And there are rumors."

"Spit it out, Jed. I'm dog tired, and I don't have time."

"What of them?" Jed jerked his thumb in the direction of Slocum and Lee.

"Not much you can say that would surprise them," Earhart said.

"Rumor has it the Goodes kidnapped him, that they've got him hid somewhere and are torturin' him!"

"Now why would they do a thing like that?" asked the sheriff. Slocum had his own thoughts on the matter. From all he had seen, the Goode family was capable of doing well-nigh anything. If this Altman had crossed them, he might be lucky he wasn't cut down out of hand.

"It's that devil Jose Espalin," Jed said. "He's got them all fired up and thinkin' Perry done them wrong."

"Range war," muttered Earhart. "Reason doesn't matter. At the bottom of this well is water rights. The Goodes don't have it, the Stuarts do. Those Texican bastards think they got a right to own this whole place."

"Get George to the undertaker's," Oliver Lee said to Jed. "And let's go get Perry while we might still find him alive."

A small crowd had gathered around the horse weighed down with McDonald's body. It took only a few minutes before a dozen men had found horses and were ready to ride.

"Where are we going?" Slocum asked the sheriff.

"Danged if I know."

"*We* do, Sheriff," called one of the men. "John Goode's always braggin' about takin' his garbage out to Swing Rock."

Earhart squinted and saw the sun poking up over the horizon. "It'll be hotter 'n Hades in an hour. Let's get out there and see if we can't do something about Altman."

"What if he's dead too?" asked Slocum. "You ready to take on the entire Goode clan?"

"Won't have any choice. What worries me more is Jed saying Jose Espalin is behind this. He's a bad one. Never does anything, but he's always goading and pushing and prodding till something bad happens. I swear, his papa must have been a vulture."

"Never kills anything but always waits for it to die," Slocum said. He had seen men like this Espalin all too often. With him tossed into the stew pot with the Goode family, the mix could be deadly.

"Don't rightly know what he gets out of stirrin' up trouble, though," Earhart said. "He rides with the Goodes, but he doesn't work for them. He and Walter Goode get drunk together, but I never saw Espalin pay for a single drink. Figured that was the attraction."

Slocum mounted and turned his tired sorrel's face in the direction of the posse already jostling and poking at one another, ready for a necktie party. If they found Perry Altman dead, they would string up any Goode they came across, guilty or not. In spite of himself, Slocum rubbed his own gritty neck.

If the posse didn't find a Goode soon enough, they might turn on any outsider. No matter that he had convinced the sheriff he was innocent of killing McDonald and knew nothing of this Altman. He was an outsider and therefore suspect.

"Don't do it, Slocum," Earhart said in a low voice, riding up to him.

"What's that, Sheriff?"

"You hightail it now, and they'll fall on you like a pack of rabid dogs."

Slocum nodded. He had reached the same conclusion. They rode on in silence until the sun was halfway up to zenith. Slocum didn't have to be told they had reached Swing Rock. The outline of the rocky formation against the sky looked like a child's swing.

"Any sign of the Goodes?" asked Earhart. No answer. He turned to Slocum. "You want to ride ahead and see if we're sticking our heads into an ambush? You have the look of a scout about you, Slocum."

"I've done that in my day," Slocum said, glad to be away from both the lawman and the posse. The men were getting itchy trigger fingers, wanting to kill something and not finding anyone handy. Slocum would rather play with old dynamite than remain with the nervous men one instant longer.

"I'll ride with you," Oliver Lee volunteered. "If I won't get in the way."

"Come on," Slocum said, knowing it wouldn't do any good to shoo the man off. "There's not too many ways up into that rock fall. You cover my back, and I'll see what I can find."

They rode a mile closer, then dismounted. Slocum drew his rifle and tossed it to Lee, who grabbed it. The man levered a round into the chamber, then nodded brusquely, showing he was ready.

Slocum set off, staying low and worrying Lee might get spooked and shoot him from behind. When he reached the narrow trail leading into the rocks, he had decided Oliver Lee was a good man to have behind him. Lee had settled down and proved almost as quiet walking through the brush as Slocum.

Motioning for Lee to stay put, Slocum made his way up the trail. He checked for spoor and found plenty. Rock had been scratched and patches of dust had been kicked up, as if someone had put up a fight while being dragged uphill.

Perry Altman? Slocum could only guess. He left the trail and edged closer to the top of the trail, stopping only when he heard low moans. Slocum fell flat on his belly and drew his six-shooter. Wiggling like a snake, he moved closer to a small hollow.

A booted foot came into view. Slocum watched as the foot kicked feebly. More moans. Slocum waited for someone to show himself, but nothing happened.

Then, from down the trail, he heard a commotion and knew instinctively what was going on. The posse had gotten antsy and decided to launch a frontal assault on this rocky citadel, no matter what might happen to Perry Altman.

Slocum took a deep breath, cursed, cocked his six-shooter, cursed again, and then blasted from his hiding place to confront Perry Altman's hidden captors before they had the chance to get their weapons out and firing.

7

Slocum stumbled and fell, sliding down the small incline to where he saw the boots kicking feebly. Swinging around, gun leveled and ready for use, Slocum found no one but a man stripped to the waist and staked out spread-eagle on the ground.

"Where are they?" Slocum demanded.

"Goode, he done this to me," moaned the prisoner.

"You Perry Altman?"

Slocum got a weak nod as reply.

"They gone? Goode and the men who did this to you?" Slocum turned, alert for the slightest sound or movement. He didn't trust the bound man to give accurate answers, not in his condition. Slocum had seen the Apaches do worse to a man—but not by much.

"All gone. Hours back. Don't know who all was here. They did terrible things." Altman began sobbing again, and

59

Slocum didn't much blame him. The man's skin had been peeled back in places, leaving bloody patches. The insects had begun their work, hungrily eating the man's flesh from his bones.

Slocum considered a single bullet between the man's eyes to put him out of his misery, but then he reconsidered. Altman might not be as bad off as he seemed.

Panting, shouting, and cursing, several of the posse burst into sight waving their six-shooters around wildly.

"Put the guns away," Slocum ordered. "This man needs help, not to be plugged by some damn fool with a wild hair up his ass."

"Settle down, Slocum," called Sheriff Earhart. "They're not gonna shoot anyone, are you, boys?" The sharp edge to the words cut through the frenzy of the hunt. The posse milled around a few seconds, then became directionless, bumping into each other and taking out their frustration in minor ways.

"Perry!" Oliver Lee pushed past Slocum and dropped beside the bound man. "Was it Walter Goode who did this to you?"

"His pa—it was John Goode!" Altman rasped out.

"Free him," Slocum ordered. No one had noticed Altman was still bound and in pain from the way he lay, bare back pressing down into the rocky ground. When no one moved, Slocum reached behind to the sheath thrust into his gunbelt and found the handle of his knife. Two swift slashes cut the rawhide strips on Altman's wrists. It took a few more minutes to get him free of the bonds around his ankles. Slocum didn't want to damage the fancy hand-tooled boots any more than he had to while setting the man free. Let him be buried in his boots, if need be.

"Give him water, help him, do something!" came the furor from the posse. They had done nothing for several minutes, and now they all wanted to help.

"Let him speak, dammit!" shouted Sheriff Earhart. "Tell us what happened, Perry."

"I—I was on my way up to George's place when I came across a half dozen of them owlhoots. They were all liquored up. I tried to get past them, but they grabbed me."

"Did you provoke them?" Earhart asked sternly.

"I don't take the kind of talk they was spoutin' off no man!" raged Altman, his fire coming back. He rubbed circulation into his cut wrists, and moaned when one man in the posse poured liquor from a hip flask over the worst of his cuts and insect bites.

"Why were you heading for McDonald's cabin?"

"I had news for him," Altman replied to Slocum. "We was supposed to finish roundin' up the strays by noon. Mr. Stuart wanted all his hands in to the ranch house for a meeting."

"Range war," grumbled Earhart, muttering under his breath so only Slocum overheard. "They nabbed you and brought you right up here?" the sheriff asked in a louder voice.

Slocum had figured out enough of what happened not to need Altman's confirmation. Wandering around the small level area set in front of the hollow in the rock, Slocum found evidence of a half-dozen men. Were any of them the pair who had bushwhacked George McDonald? Slocum doubted it. To ride back here and get Altman into the condition he was in would have required horses able to race faster than the wind. From Altman's appearance, John Goode had taken some time and enjoyed his bloody handiwork.

John Goode had probably intercepted Altman while two others—his son Walter and another—were back-shooting McDonald.

"What did they want to know?" Slocum asked suddenly.

"What?" Earhart frowned and glared at Slocum. "What are you asking?"

"They could have cut him down in the saddle when they first spotted him. They might have strung him up. There's more than one cottonwood tall enough between the line shack and this place. If they didn't kill him, they wanted something from him. What?"

"Well, Perry, what did Goode ask?"

Perry Altman bit his lower lip and looked like he wanted to die.

"Tell us, you mangy son of a bitch. You done something wrong, didn't you, Altman?" shouted one of the posse.

"I couldn't help myself. I was afeared for my life. The pain! You'll never know what it was like!"

"What did they asked?" repeated Sheriff Earhart.

"They ast about the womenfolk. They wanted to know how many there were, if they had children, about their husbands. And I tole them! I tole them everything!"

"Why'd they want to know all that?" asked Oliver Lee, puzzled. "Unless they mean to harm them!"

This revelation brought cries of anger to the lips of the posse. Half were already starting for their horses tethered at the bottom of the rise. The others demanded more information—and more than one wanted to up and leave Perry Altman where he was for his weakness.

"Reckon they mean business," Slocum said. "Can't believe a man would harm another's woman, even in a blood feud."

"Them Texans are more than mean. They are downright despicable," said Lee. His hand went to his holstered six-gun and tapped the butt. He was ready to kill any of the Goode family he got in his sights, and Slocum understood his feeling. The man had forced the bullet found near

McDonald's body through a watch chain on his vest. Oliver Lee carried that slug like some symbol of death—or revenge.

"Everybody back to Tularosa," cried Sheriff Earhart. "We got a wounded man to tend to." Three of the posse helped Perry Altman to his feet. He could hardly walk, and they ended up half-carrying, half-dragging him down the slope.

"We need to do more 'n that," Altman said. "We need to get the women on a train out of here."

"Next train's due this afternoon," Oliver Lee said. "But it's going to El Paso. We ought to consider that."

"We can defend their honor," Earhart said, glaring at Altman. Slocum knew the sheriff didn't appreciate having his competence challenged like this. Altman was openly saying the lawman was not capable of maintaining the law and protecting innocent women.

"That's safer for 'em than here," countered Altman. "If they can jump me like this, they might do terrible things to our women. You can't be everywhere all the time, Sheriff. There's too many of them varmints to fight."

"The law is everywhere there're law-abiding citizens," Earhart said. Slocum saw the ripple of tension pass throughout the posse. What the lawman had wanted to say was immediately changed in every man's mind. Earhart had just condoned vigilante action, and couldn't get the sentence shoved back down his own throat.

A cheer went up. The posse mounted and started toward town. Slocum hung back, deciding what to do. He found himself riding alongside Lee and Perry Altman, who wobbled as he clung to the other man just to stay in the saddle.

"Slocum, we don't know you or know much about you, but we'd appreciate it if you'd do us a favor."

"What?" Slocum didn't want to hear what Altman was asking.

"Would you escort the women to El Paso for us? I don't know there's a man here what would want to leave with the Goodes running wild like they are."

"I might be better used tracking down McDonald's killer." Slocum knew he ought to stay clear of the squabble that was building into an all-out shooting war. But heading back to El Paso with a trainload of women wasn't to his liking.

He wasn't sure tracking down the men who killed George McDonald was either, but it struck him as a more productive use of his time. And there was always a chance he could simply ride off and let the law handle the hunt for Walter Goode and his unknown sidekick.

"Not been the same since them Texans came here, no, sir," grumbled Altman. "They do things like torture me—and kill George. Can't believe he's gone. Them murderin' bastards!"

"Beeves have been vanishing too," said Oliver Lee. "We always lost one or two now and again to the Apaches whenever they passed through, but since the Goodes came to Tularosa, we been losing ten, twenty, and more every week."

"Have you checked their herds to see if they're running your brands?" asked Slocum.

"Of course. They complain about losing from their own herds, but what else would you expect from them? They're liars, each and every one of them." Oliver Lee spat to show his disgust with the newcomers.

Slocum rode in silence for a mile or two, mulling over all he had heard. He wished he could talk with John Goode for a spell, to see what the Texan had to say. With the man so eager to use his six-shooter, Slocum knew that wasn't likely to happen.

And there was no doubt who had caught Altman and tortured him. The small information gained was out of proportion to what the Goodes had done to the man, and that bothered Slocum. Being cruel because they enjoyed it made the Goode family a loose cannon rolling around and ready to fire in unknown directions.

And Slocum had to admit the evidence lay square against Walter Goode in the murder of George McDonald. The man had been unarmed, and there had been two bushwhackers.

"The train," called Oliver Lee. "It's just now pulling into the station!"

They picked up the pace. Perry Altman hung on, more unconscious than aware. Slocum put his heels to his sorrel's flanks and went ahead. Too much was happening in Tularosa for any of the posse to remember that Altman needed the doctor. He dropped to the ground in front of the doctor's office and saw Doc Benoit asleep on his desk, arms crossed and head on them.

"Wake up, Doc!" Slocum bellowed. The drunken doctor snapped upright, appearing almost sober for a moment.

"What can I do for you, sir?"

"Perry Altman's been badly wounded. Get ready to fix him up. Oliver Lee's bringing him in. They're not ten minutes behind me." Slocum paused, then added, "You might want to pour a pot of coffee down your gullet to burn off some of that rotgut."

"I am able to operate, sir. How dare you!"

"If he doesn't walk out of here an hour after you start on him, I'll need the undertaker."

"He will not die in my care, sir."

"The undertaker'd be for you," Slocum said coldly. The shock sobered the man more than a pot of hot, strong coffee ever could. Slocum went outside in time to help get Altman into the surgery.

"Never seen Doc like this in the middle of the day," Lee said when they got Altman stretched out.

"Drunk?" asked Slocum, hardly believing it.

"Nope, sober. His hands aren't even shaking. Maybe he's turned over a new leaf."

Slocum snorted.

"Come on, men. They're getting the women on the train bound for El Paso," someone shouted from the street. Lee and Slocum walked the short distance to the edge of town. A dozen women huddled together fearfully, a small pile of carpetbags and trunks waiting to be loaded into the baggage car. The men with them stood in another small knot, fingering rifles and making occasional loud noises as they worked themselves up to a fever pitch.

Slocum was worried that he might be on the receiving end of the gathering vigilante group, but then Sheriff Earhart strode onto the platform, his thumbs tucked into his gunbelt. The bantam rooster of a lawman looked around, then spoke in a loud, clear voice.

"Ladies, I don't see any reason for you to go gallivanting off to El Paso, but if that's what your husbands and menfolks want, I hope you have a pleasant trip. Just be sure to plan on returning real soon. Tularosa needs your beauty and feminine touch to keep civilization alive here. All these ornery galoots are proof of that!"

"A pretty speech, Sheriff. What you plannin' in doing about the Goodes?" someone in the crowd called. The cocking of rifles and the whisper of six-shooters coming out of holsters sounded like thunder to Slocum.

Slocum took a step away from Oliver Lee and started down the railroad depot steps. He could be out of town by the time anyone noticed he was gone. He could get back up into the Sacramento Mountains and find Angelina. He remembered his brief tryst with the Aztec priestess, and wanted more of what the lovely woman had to offer. She was brave, and undeniably commanding.

And she might be the key to finding a mine stuffed full of gold coins.

"The ladies will make the trip to El Paso just fine without an escort," Earhart said. "Slocum will help scout to find the men who killed George McDonald."

All eyes turned to Slocum, pinning him to the spot. He knew better than to back out now, confronted by angry men wanting to string up anyone who crossed them.

A cheer went up, and Slocum knew he would have to make other plans to find Angelina and the gold guarded by her serpent god.

8

"There's no doubt Goode's hightailed it?" Slocum asked the sheriff.

Earhart shook his head, wiped sweat from his face with his bandanna, then said, "Jed's not the brightest man around, but he's smart enough to ask questions."

"And everyone's willing to help out," Perry Altman said. The man was covered with patches of white plaster and bandages, looking like he'd wrapped himself in a big hurry. Slocum figured the doctor had wasted no time slathering on anything he could find, then winding bandages around to appease Slocum.

"You figure it might be anyone else but Walter Goode who killed McDonald?" Slocum knew the answer, but wanted to weasel out of going with the posse if he could. From the ring of expectant faces around him, he realized that wasn't possible. He had not accompanied their women to El

Paso. That meant he'd ride with them to track down Walter
Goode and bring him to justice.

This caused Slocum some irritation. He never cottoned
much to lynch mobs. He had been on the receiving end of
their wrath—and their ropes—too many times. Being the one
putting the noose over another man's head was better than
dangling from the hemp necktie himself, but that didn't mean
Slocum enjoyed being a part of it. From all he had seen and
heard and gleaned from the place where McDonald had been
gunned down, Walter Goode was the varmint responsible.

Goode and the mysterious man riding with him.

"Tell me more about this Jose Espalin," Slocum asked
the sheriff. "He come to town with the Goode family or is
he a drifter?"

Earhart looked to Jed, then to the others around him. Then
he shrugged. "He's as mean as they come. He'd as soon
knife you in the back as look at you. Then he'd laugh about
it. Don't know if he works for the Goodes or just runs with
that pack of wolves."

"Heard tell he hired on with them right after they come
here," one man in the posse piped up. "Espalin came in
from over in Arizona Territory. Yuma, maybe."

"But he and Walter Goode hit it off right from the start,"
Perry Altman said. "They're always together. If you step on
one's toes, the other says ouch."

Slocum thought about this while the men boasted and
bragged and told each other what they'd do when they caught
up with the Goode clan. He didn't take this as a favorable
sign the men would obey the sheriff once they caught scent
of their quarry. At least Sheriff Earhart realized there would
be problems controlling the unruly bunch.

"None of that, men," Earhart said sternly. "This is a duly
deputized, legal posse, not a lynch mob. We'll capture Goode
and return him to town to stand trial. When we hang the son

of a bitch, it's going to be after a jury finds him guilty!''

The posse took this as a rallying cry. They started shouting, "String 'im up, string 'im up!''

"You got a problem with them, Sheriff," Slocum said
softly.

"You're going to be scouting in front of them. I'd say
you better watch your back and be damn good at tracking.''

"You mean I'd better find Goode," Slocum said.

Earhart's crooked smile left no room for doubt about what
he intended.

A half hour later, loaded down with water and supplies,
they set off for McDonald's line shack, then got on the trail
after Goode and his henchman.

"We gotta find water, Slocum," pleaded one of the posse.
"We been ridin' for a solid week and ain't found a drop in
the last two days.''

"You got water yesterday," Slocum pointed out. His own
mouth had turned into the inside of a cotton bale. He rolled
a small stone around in the Apache fashion, but this worked
for only so long. They all needed to find water fast, or they
would die under the burning New Mexico sun. How Walter
Goode had lasted this long to lead them smack into the badlands was beyond Slocum.

It was almost as if he had intended to strand any posse
out here in the Mal Pais.

White gypsum crunched under Slocum's horse's hooves
as he walked the sorrel, hunting for tracks. He worked more
on instinct than any real spoor. He had found fresh horse
dung a few miles back, and had taken it into his head that
this was the proper path. Truth was, the horse leaving the
pile could have gone in about any direction that didn't take
it back into the posse. The rider might have been an hour
ahead or even five. It was hard for Slocum to concentrate.

In the badlands hardly anything grew above waist-high. Here and there greasewood popped up through the sunbaked ground, and more than a few mesquites dropped their roots a hundred feet into cool earth to find water. Slocum was at the point of digging down and following those taproots to even a drop of moisture.

"We ought to turn back," Earhart said. "We been out too long. We'll never find Goode." His tone made Slocum bristle. The sheriff made it sound as if it was his fault they had not overtaken the outlaw yet.

"He's been keeping up a fast pace, as if he wanted to avoid a posse intent on stringing him up," Slocum said coldly. "That has more to do with it than anything else. Unless you mean not having water, tracking through white sand, getting our heads roasted by this infernal sun—"

"Enough, Slocum, enough. We're all getting edgy." Earhart wiped sweat from his sunburned face. "Turning back's no better than going on to see this manhunt through."

"I agree. We're likely to find water if we keep riding. We know there's nothing behind us," Slocum said. From the way his sorrel nervously stepped, tossing her head and occasionally tugging at the reins he held so loosely in his hands, he figured she might smell water.

He gave the sorrel her head and pretended he thought this would really lead to water. When he topped a rocky sand dune, he blinked, thinking he was seeing a mirage.

"We're saved!" cried several in the posse. They had been dragging along minutes before, but now they saw an oasis in the middle of the badlands. A small shack leaned precariously away from the prevailing hot desert wind, but the real treat lay in the pump standing outside. A pump meant water.

Or did it? Slocum knew water was scarce in these parts, and the shack might have been abandoned because the well ran dry. There was only one way to find out if the dried-out water trough could be filled using the pump.

He intended to start pumping like hell.

Slipping and sliding down the steep, sandy embankment brought him to a rockier patch. Here and there he saw where cottonwoods had grown once. Whoever built the shack had cut the lot of them down to use as walls and roof. Adobe would have been a better choice out in the middle of the Mal Pais, but Slocum had long since given up figuring why men did what they did.

There was nothing but sizzling death to be found out here. Who had built the cabin and why would remain a secret forever. But if there was water underground, Slocum would never once question why providence had brought him in this direction.

"Pump, damn you, pump!" cried Jed.

"Hold on," Slocum cautioned. "The sucker washer might be old. Break it and you'll never get a drop pulled up."

"Lookee here!" Jed said, falling to his knees. He lifted a glass jar filled with water.

"Hold it," Slocum ordered. His command came with all the snap and authority of the captain he had been in the CSA. "There's a note stuck to the jaw. What's it say?"

Jed held it up so Slocum could read it.

"Says the water is to soften the sucker washer. Don't drink the water, pour it into the pump. Then we can get all the water we can use."

"No, no," Jed said, his hand drifting to his six-shooter. "I want this water. I got a powerful bad thirst."

"Jed," Sheriff Earhart said. "Give me the water."

"Sheriff, you always were a goldanged fool when it came to stayin' alive. I—"

He never got any farther. Slocum walked up and drew his Colt Navy, using the barrel to smash the man's head. He sank down. Slocum grabbed the jar before Jed dropped it. The deputy moaned and thrashed about feebly on the ground, but Slocum paid him no heed. Stepping over him, he went to the pump and looked at the others in the posse.

"Any objections?" he asked. The six-shooter still in one hand and the water jar in the other, Slocum waited until he was sure no one was going to complain.

He laid down his six-gun and then twisted off the tight-fitting lid. A few drops of the water sloshed into his leathery skin. Soft, wet, compelling. He wanted to drink the hot water. It had been a full day since he'd had enough water in his mouth to even whistle. How could he know the note wasn't a lie? When had the water been left? The washer might be broken, and pouring the water in would only return the water to its origins deep underground.

"Faith, Slocum," Earhart said. "That's what it all comes down to. Do you believe in the goodness of your fellow man?"

"No," Slocum said. And then he poured the water into the pump. Grabbing the handle, he jerked it up and down as hard and fast as he could. For an agonizing few seconds he thought nothing was happening. Then he felt resistance and heard a gurgling sound deep under his feet.

The first geyser of water from the pump came out brown and dirty. Every subsequent pump brought up cleaner, sweeter water. He kept pumping while the rest of the posse fell face-first into the trough and drank their fill. Only when a few had backed off, bellies bloating like foolish horses, did Slocum plunge his head into the tepid water.

It was warm, and he would never have asked for a glass of it if he had been in a town of any size. But he was so parched his lips cracked. He sucked in water, sputtered, and then started drinking.

"One thing we know," Earhart said after a spell, "is that Walter Goode didn't come this way."

"He wouldn't have left the jar full for us to find," Slocum said. Even as he spoke, he filled the glass jar and screwed down the top. The note was returned to its spot on the outside for the next dehydrated traveler to find and use.

"Where now, Slocum?"

"We were heading in yonder direction," Slocum said, pointing to the line of travel they had followed since he had found the horse dung. "No reason we shouldn't go back that way and see what we can find."

"You don't have any idea where Goode is, do you?" asked Jed, still rubbing the side of his head where Slocum had buffaloed him. "You're a danged fraud, Slocum. You—"

"Jed," Earhart said softly. "Slocum used his pistol barrel on the side of your head. You keep on like that and I'll use mine on the top of your empty head."

"But Sheriff, he . . ."

Earhart was short but determined. He puffed up and banged his chest against the much larger man. Jed backed down, grumbling.

"Wouldn't turn your back on him, Slocum. He's taken a powerful dislike to you, even if you did save us all from dying of thirst," opined Sheriff Earhart.

"Hard not to expose my back if I'm scouting," Slocum said. He let his sorrel have some more of the water, then mounted and rode slowly away, heading in the direction his sixth sense told him was the proper one. He was aware of Jed's hot gaze on him, but he ignored it. He had enough water now, and though his belly grumbled from lack of food, he felt better than he had in days. Along with this went a confidence that he was getting close to his quarry.

"Ride where you want, you son of a bitch," Slocum said

softly to Walter Goode, "but you can't hide forever. I'm going to find you."

Slocum almost rode past Walter Goode near sundown. He was hidden in deep shadows cast by the tall sand dunes and jagged rock.

Grabbing for his Colt, Slocum relaxed when he saw that Goode wasn't moving. The man lay as if wrapped in his bedroll, but even through the cloaking shadow, Slocum saw there wasn't anything to worry over. Walter Goode wasn't likely to throw down on him.

Walter Goode wasn't likely to do much of anything. He was stone dead.

Slocum dismounted and let his sorrel move away from the body. Studying the ground as he approached, he tried to figure out what had happened. The shifting gypsum and stony patches kept him from finding tracks—any tracks, including Goode's.

The man lay on his side, face buried in the sand. He had bled a mite from the bullet wound in his forehead, but not much. Ants worked away at the body, but hadn't made much progress. Slocum guessed Goode hadn't been dead more than six hours. A small-caliber six-gun lay near the body.

"What happened, Slocum?" said Sheriff Earhart querulously.

"Looks like he shot himself," Slocum said. The sheriff came up. The rest of the posse trickled in, arriving in twos and threes.

"The bastard cheated us!" cried Jed. "I wanted to put the rope around his worthless neck myself! Might still do it. Don't matter none if he's already dead, does it?"

Slocum ignored the deputy and picked up the fallen gun. He held it out for Oliver Lee's inspection. The man tugged at the watch chain and got the slug he had found near George McDonald's body. The lead fit perfectly into the barrel.

"Same caliber," Lee said. He opened the cylinder and checked the rounds. "Three rounds fired. This is the gun, Sheriff. He killed McDonald and then shot himself when it looked like he'd be caught."

"Or maybe he was dying of thirst," said Perry Altman. "We danged near died ourselves."

"Only three rounds fired?" Slocum asked. "And he never reloaded in eight days since killing McDonald? Does that make sense?"

"Maybe he didn't have any spare ammo," someone suggested. "Let's find his horse and check his saddlebags to find out."

"Good idea," Slocum allowed. He frowned and stared at the body. "Sheriff, if a man blew his own brains out, would he put the gun to the middle of his forehead? Or would he stick the gun to the side of his head?"

"Can't rightly say what would go through a man like Goode's mind before he killed himself."

"Ever shoot a man up close, Sheriff?" Slocum asked.

"Once or twice," Earhart said. He chuckled. "Even set fire to one man's coat. That did more to stop him than the bullet."

"Lot of gunpowder comes out the muzzle, even for a small-caliber six-shooter," Slocum said. "There's no powder on his forehead."

"What are you saying, Slocum?"

"Looks to me like someone else shot him, maybe from a couple feet away, then dropped the gun so we'd think Goode killed himself."

"Hey, Sheriff, we got the horse. It was hobbling over the rise," shouted a posse member.

Slocum and Earhart tramped through the sand to find the horse, all skin and bones and hardly able to stand due to exposure and dehydration. Dropping down, Slocum grabbed the skittish animal's leg and pulled it up. A festering wound showed where the spine of a Spanish bayonet cactus had gouged deep into the forelock.

"If this is Goode's horse," Slocum said, "I'd say we ran down a killer. The horse is injured just as I'd said it would be."

"That's enough to convince me," the lawman said. He drew his six-shooter and told Slocum, "Stand back. Even if this is Goode's horse, I can't stand to see it suffer one second longer."

The gunshot echoed across the badlands and faded swiftly. The horse let out a single loud snort that was almost one of relief, then sank to the ground, as dead as its owner. Slocum and Earhart returned to Goode's body, and saw it slung over the back of Jed's horse so they could take it back to Tularosa.

Walter Goode had met his maker—but at whose hand?

Slocum grew increasingly uneasy as they rode back to town with the body, the others in the posse bragging about bagging their quarry and whipping themselves up into a frenzy against the man they knew to be their real enemy.

John Goode.

The hatred would never stop until a full-scale range war burned it out of them.

9

Tularosa had never looked better to Slocum as he rode into town, the posse scattered around him. He was tired, thirsty, and ready to sleep for a week. The only question in his mind was whether to eat a big meal and drink his fill before going to the town's single hotel and finding a flea-infested room, or just hunt up the hotel and worry about food later, after a long night's sleep.

"Go on, men," Sheriff Earhart called, his energy seemingly fed by the return to his town. "Get the body over to the undertaker's. Jed, you figure out how to tell John Goode about his son."

"Me, Sheriff? Why me? That son of a bitch will gun down anyone tellin' him news like this! I want a dozen of the posse to go with me. They're still deputized!"

"If a herd of deputies rides into his barnyard," Slocum

said, "Goode's going to start shooting first and listen later. If he ever does."

"Jed's got a point, though." Earhart laughed derisively. "About the only time he does is when his own hide's in danger of gettin' ventilated. He rides to the Goode ranch, and he would never come back."

As dog tired as Slocum was and as ornery as Jed was, Slocum saw nothing wrong with this.

"You folks settle it, Sheriff," Slocum said tiredly. "I've done my duty as I see it. I'm ready for a drink or two, a plate heaping with food, and some sleep."

Earhart started to complain, to say that he wanted Slocum to deliver the bad news to the Texan. Then he subsided. Slocum didn't care who told Goode about his son Walter. He was glad to wash his hands of the whole affair, though some parts still bothered him.

Walter Goode had not killed himself. Whoever had ridden with him when he had killed George McDonald was responsible. Maybe the same man had killed both McDonald and Goode. Slocum turned and watched them pull Goode's body from the back of a horse and frowned. The man had short legs. He remembered the saddle on the horse with the Spanish bayonet gouge in its leg. The stirrups had been set for a man with longer legs.

Might be that Goode had nothing to do with McDonald's killing and had somehow stumbled on the real killer. Slocum shook his head, brushed off dry dust from his black Stetson, and went into the saloon to wet his whistle.

"You have the look of a man needing food too," the barkeep said. Slocum was exhausted and had been arguing with himself over food or sleep. The bartender settled the matter. The way Slocum's belly growled would have kept him awake.

"One of everything," Slocum said, reaching into his pocket to pull out a greenback. He touched the vest pocket where the Aztec coin rode next to his watch. And inside his shirt the green feather tickled his bare skin.

Too many things demanded his time and attention. He wished he had never found the gold coin, or the green feather Angelina thought belonged to her feathered serpent god Quetzalcoatl, that he had never run afoul of the Goodes or been dragooned into helping Sheriff Earhart. Tularosa had not smiled favorably on him.

A crooked grin came to his lips. The time spent with Angelina wasn't so bad, he decided as he munched on the sandwich dropped in front of him. A bowl of stew contained pieces of meat he couldn't identify. Slocum didn't care if it was chunks of skunk and boiled vulture beak. He wolfed it all down as if it were tasty. Then he finished with three warm beers that made him belch.

"Another," he called to the barkeep.

"What? Food or beer?"

Slocum considered for a moment, then said, "Both."

Before the bartender could deliver the new plate and mug, Sheriff Earhart and two deputies came swinging through the doors. Slocum considered running for the back door. If he was lucky, he could be out of town before they caught him.

"Slocum!" The tone made Slocum think about drawing. He was imprisoned in Tularosa as surely as if the sheriff had him locked up in the town jail.

"I don't want to be part of the posse any longer," Slocum said. "I just want to leave. I was on my way to Santa Fe."

"This is on the way—and you're still deputized as a member of my posse. You know the penalty for turning tail when I give a command."

"This isn't the army," Slocum said.

"You can be in my hoosegow for a long time waiting for

the judge to make his circuit through town. Might be a month or more,'' Earhart said.

"What's wrong now?''

"Got a report of John Goode and some of his men shooting up Oliver Lee's ranch. The folks still there are in a bad way.''

"Why'd he do a fool thing like that? Did he hear about his son already?''

Earhart shook his head. "Best I can tell, he thought Walter's body was being hid out there and wanted it. We were riding into town with the corpse about that time, so John Goode's reactin' to rumors, not cold facts.''

"Nothing's cold in Tularosa,'' Slocum complained. He wiped sweat from his forehead, as much from the stifling heat as from the position Earhart had put him in.

"The range war is heating up,'' Earhart agreed. The short sheriff tucked his thumbs in his gunbelt and hitched up his shooting iron. The action told Slocum as much about Earhart and his intentions as anything else. The sheriff would fight to the death to keep the peace—and he would do it against anyone breaking the law.

"So what can I do that you can't? You're the elected sheriff,'' Slocum said.

"I need men backing me up, men I can trust,'' Earhart said, his expression changing a mite. For the first time, the feisty lawman spoke with a hint of pleading in his tone.

"All right, but this is going to be it,'' Slocum said. "I'm moving on after things get settled.''

"Thanks, Slocum.'' Earhart nodded briskly, whirled around, and left, his boot heels clicking loudly on the wooden floor. Slocum drained his beer and grabbed the sandwich, stuffing it into his mouth as he went to find his horse.

• • •

"I'm worried, Slocum," Oliver Lee said. "Something's wrong. Too quiet by half."

"It's been hours since Goode came by. He's bound to have moved on." Slocum glanced around. Half the posse had left a mile down the road. He wasn't sure where they'd gone, but he had forced back a notion to join them and then simply drift off.

"He left bodies behind. My cousin's in there. Thank the Lord we sent the womenfolk to El Paso. Goode would have murdered them."

"You don't know what's gone on here," Slocum said. His keen eyes worked over the dusty yard in front of the ranch house. Nothing stirred. Nothing.

"Slocum, take a gander at this. Must be a pile of spent cartridges a foot high," called the sheriff. Slocum rode over and shook his head. Whoever had stood there hadn't been too mindful of rationing his ammo. The spent brass was deep enough to hide the ground from sight. "Must be a hundred rounds or more."

"I'll scout the place to see if it's safe," Slocum said. "Lee, you watch my back and make sure nobody gets too antsy." He glanced at Jed. The deputy fingered his six-shooter as if he wanted to open up, although there wasn't anyone to shoot at.

"I understand, Slocum," Lee said. "And thanks for doing this. You want anything, it's yours. You're a real friend."

Slocum grunted. He didn't want to be friends with either side in this fight. Best he could tell, the local ranchers hated John Goode because he was an arrogant son of a bitch—and was rich and from Texas. There might be other reasons for the animosity, and Slocum did not doubt they existed after seeing what Goode had done to Perry Altman, but when men started dying it was time to call it quits, get to the bottom of the feud, and cut it out like a nettle.

Dropping to the ground, Slocum loosened his Colt in its holster, slipping off the leather keeper from the hammer. He did not draw, however, as he bent double and made a quick dash for the barn. He had the feeling someone had kept him in his sights the entire way, but he couldn't figure who it might be.

With a swift move, he spun around the door and burst into the barn. A few frightened squawks from chickens running loose was all the response he got. The horses were gone. Here and there dusty trails caused by bullet holes in the walls letting in sunlight showed how many bullets had been pumped through the building.

But the silence told the story. Nothing human lived inside.

Slocum moved on quickly, going to the far side of the barn and sliding over a windowsill like a snake slithering toward its hole. Staying low, Slocum made his way to the water trough. So many bullets had cut through the wooden trough, they had drained its contents. The water and dirt mix had long since turned to dry, caked mud. It crunched under his weight as he worked forward.

Slocum got a good look at the ranch house and saw the few glass windows had been blown out. What held his attention, though, was the glint of sunlight off a rifle barrel.

Had the posse inadvertently trapped Goode and his cohorts inside the house after the Texans killed Lee's family? He fancied how the man might be crouching inside, waiting in ambush to potshot the sheriff and everyone with him.

Then Slocum got a hold on his imagination. There was no evidence of that. Where were Goode's horses? Those in the barn were missing. And John Goode would have ridden into the ranch on horseback. If someone in the house waited for others to ride up, it wasn't likely to be Goode.

Moving as soft as any shadow, Slocum made his way to the side of the house. Rather than venture a look into the ranch house through the window where the rifle barrel poked out, he pressed his face against the adobe and tried to peer through a crack caused by a half-dozen bullets blowing away the mud brick.

He saw nothing moving, but he saw nothing to hint there weren't a dozen men with their horses waiting inside either.

Slocum waved to the sheriff to let him know he had decided to go in. Oliver Lee appeared nervous and likely to do something foolish if Slocum didn't find out what was going on fast.

With footsteps like a cat's, Slocum made his way around to the back. He jumped and caught a beam sticking out of the adobe, and pulled himself onto the roof. A half-dozen spots had been charred, as if torches had been tossed but had sputtered out quickly.

"Fresh," Slocum said, rubbing the ash between his fingers. Goode had tried to burn out those inside, but had failed. Dropping flat onto the roof, Slocum began scrabbling to push apart the burned sections. He opened a hole the size of his head. Taking a deep breath, he hazarded a quick look down into the dim interior. Then he pulled back fast and stood. He took off his hat and waved.

"Sheriff, get on in here. Man's wounded bad, maybe dead!"

Oliver Lee beat the lawman to the front door by a dozen yards. He hit the ground running and burst into the main room. Slocum swung down and followed him.

"Matt, Matt, are you all right? Oh, Matt, I'll see those owlhoots at the end of a rope for this!"

"Uncle Ollie," came the weak reply. "I fought 'em as long as I could. So many bullets."

"Don't talk."

"They killed Sundown. Shot him down where he stood." Matt coughed up some blood, but Slocum didn't think the lung had been punctured. There wasn't any pink froth with it. And Matt was hardly more than thirteen or fourteen, but big for his age. John Goode had shot a boy, even if the boy had a rifle and had obviously used it often and well to keep the attackers at bay. Spent brass lay all around on the floor.

"Who's Sundown? Hired hand?"

"Our dog," Oliver Lee said. "Those back-shooters kilt our dog!"

"Looks like your nephew is going to make it," Slocum said. "Weak from loss of blood, but otherwise all his parts are working."

"Was there anyone else in here?" demanded Sheriff Earhart. "This the only casualty?"

"Reckon so, Sheriff," Slocum said. "Goode rode up, shot a few hundred rounds, killed the dog, then left."

"And all because he thought his boy's body was hidden under a bed," Earhart said, shaking his head. "We got a fight on our hands, Slocum. Let Oliver take care of his kin."

"Fight? Where? The place is deserted." Slocum didn't bother adding even the dog was gone.

"A couple of the men I sent off to circle round the ranch found Goode and opened up on him. He's shooting back and it looks serious."

"Matt," Slocum asked. "Are you sure it was John Goode who did all this shooting?"

The boy nodded weakly. This was indictment enough for Slocum—and more than enough for everyone else. They had wanted reason to arrest John Goode or even string him up. The attack on Oliver Lee's ranch house had given them all the argument any needed to go after him.

"Where are they?" asked Slocum. He tipped his head to one side and heard distant gunfire. Turning slowly, he homed in on it.

"They're in a wash not a mile off. The deputies happened on their camp and surprised them."

"Who was surprised? Goode or your deputies?" asked Slocum, only half joshing.

"Why, Goode, of course."

"Doesn't make a lot of sense he would shoot up the ranch house, then ride off a mile and pitch camp in the middle of the day," Slocum said. "But then, not much of what Goode's done makes one whit of sense."

They rode hard, Slocum's sorrel straining under him. The horse needed a long rest after the week in the Mal Pais retrieving Walter Goode's body and after this exhausting gallop. Slocum reined back after less than a half mile, letting the struggling horse regain its wind. More than giving the horse a rest, Slocum wanted to avoid riding smack into the middle of a fight.

"Whatcha hangin' back for, Slocum? You *want* them varmints to get away?" Jed was becoming more obnoxious by the minute. He scented a necktie party, and that put lead into his pencil.

"I want to be sure to testify against them," Slocum answered. "How's the sheriff going to attack?"

"Flat-out, full frontal assault at a gallop! Ride down their gun barrels and dare 'em to fire!" shouted Jed. Slocum wished the deputy would follow that trail. It improved everyone's chances. Not only would Goode have one less round to shoot at men with good sense, it would eliminate a thorn in the side of the posse.

"Go to it," Slocum said, veering off to circle the fight and come in from the flank. He figured it would be over quickly, one way or the other. Goode couldn't have too much ammunition left after the all-out attack on Oliver Lee's house.

As he crested a sand dune, he got a good view of the fight

going on. Three horses lay dead at the bottom of an arroyo, shot as the posse attacked Goode's camp. The Texan hadn't been caught napping, though. The man had hightailed it, firing wildly as he went. Those with John Goode formed a tight knot and fought to get a way out of the tight noose of the posse closing around them. But one rider in particular caught Slocum's eye.

Dressed in dusty black trail clothing, the man quickly separated from Goode's band and rode hard to get away. Slocum put his heels into the lathered flanks of his sorrel and took off after the fleeing man. Something drew him to chase after this one owlhoot, and he couldn't say why. There was a better chance of stopping Goode and the others with him in their small camp, but Slocum chose to run down this solitary rider.

Slocum cut loose with his six-shooter and fired a few times. The man jerked around, startled by the pursuit. Then he bent over, head down by his horse's neck, and tried to get even more speed out of an already tired horse.

Slocum fired his last three rounds, aiming the best he could, knowing that he was more likely to give speed to the fleeing man than to stop him. Still, it surprised him when the dark-clad man grabbed for his leg. Hitting him at this distance had to be closer to a miracle than a display of shooting skill. What startled Slocum even more than the notion he had winged the man at a hundred yards was the brightness flashing in the afternoon sunlight.

The sorrel flagged quickly, letting Slocum's quarry vanish over a rise. Disgusted, Slocum reined in and gave the exhausted horse a chance to catch its breath. He dismounted and bent to see what the flash had been.

He hadn't produced a flow of blood. He had unleashed a torrent of coins into the hot New Mexico desert sand. Slocum held one up and let out a low whistle when he saw the face of the coin.

Aztec gold.

10

Slocum tucked the few pieces of Aztec gold he could find into his pockets. What was the rider doing with a handful of the coins? Slocum wiped his lips and stared after the fleeing man, realizing someone had beaten him to the gold. His stray shot had cut a leather pouch holding the precious coins. Slocum would rather have brought the rider out of the saddle with his shot, but the Aztec gold he found was adequate pay for this day's work.

A half dozen joined the single coin already resting in his pocket.

"Wonder if he was the one who got careless before?" Slocum said aloud, considering the source of the piece of gold he had found in the road so long ago as he had ridden for Santa Fe. He hastily stopped his hunt for more coins when he saw Sheriff Earhart riding up. The lawman had a grim look about him. Slocum didn't have to ask to know the raid had not gone well.

"Killed three of their horses," Earhart said without preamble. He spat and shook his head. "Weren't even *their* horses. They were the ones stolen from Lee's barn."

"Goode escaped?" asked Slocum.

"The varmint got clean away. The posse tried to chase him, but their mounts were too tuckered from the ride out of town. Goode waltzed off, with not so much as a fare-thee-well to us. Catching him is going to require more time and patience than I want to spend."

Slocum knew what the sheriff meant. Tracking Goode throughout the territory would take money and men. Neither the territorial governor nor the federal marshal, wherever he might be, was likely to authorize spending money to capture John Goode.

"Think he knew his son was already dead?" asked Slocum. "That might explain why he shot up the ranch house."

"He couldn't have known. Still doesn't, is my guess," Earhart said. "I've put Jed on his trail, but that's like pouring kerosene on a fire to put it out. Jed won't do much 'cept fan the flames."

"Why not send Oliver Lee?" Slocum knew the man had a good head on his shoulders, and he was more likely to worry about what the law actually said than the deputy ever would.

"He wanted to tend his nephew. Perry Altman's too wrapped up in getting even for all Goode did to him." Earhart spat, fumbled in his shirt pocket for a plug of tobacco, bit off a hunk, then chewed and spat again. "Can't trust Lee, now that I think on it. The man's wearing the bullet used to kill his friend like some damn charm."

"Walter Goode did that deed," Slocum pointed out.

"You're no fool, Slocum. You saw what I did out there. You really think Goode killed himself? For all that, do you think he killed McDonald?"

"Don't know about McDonald, but I'd be willing to lay odds that someone riding with John Goode is likely to have killed his son."

"You were shooting at Jose Espalin," Earhart said. "I'd recognize his evil face anywhere."

"Espalin," Slocum said. "The name keeps cropping up. He work for Goode?"

"Can't say," Earhart told him. "I think so. He and Walter Goode were partners. At least they were seen together by lots of folks the past few weeks."

"What would he gain by shooting Walter Goode?" Slocum thought out loud. "For that, what would he gain by gunning down George McDonald from ambush?"

"You're thinking the same that I am, Slocum. Jose Espalin is the axle around which this whole damned infernal wheel of death turns. I have to get back to town and keep a tight lid on things. With some of the men agitating for a vigilance committee, I need to show myself to keep them quieted down."

"You won't get much support from the Stuart brothers either," Slocum guessed. Anything that rid the territory of the Goode family benefited the ranchers who were already operating there. Added range and water would be theirs again for the taking if John Goode and his kin were killed or run out of the Tularosa Basin.

"Go after Espalin," Earhart said. Again the note of begging came into his voice. Slocum knew it was hard for a proud man to ask for help from a stranger, especially one he didn't much cotton to. Sheriff Earhart had made it plain he thought Slocum was a gunman come to town to cause trouble, and now he was asking for help to do the very thing he wanted to avoid.

If Slocum came back with Espalin swung over the rump of his horse, Earhart would be the last to ask questions about what had happened, no matter how much he worked to uphold the law.

Earhart fumbled in his pocket and pulled out a battered tin star. "This is the only spare I've got. Jed's wearing the other one." He held it out for Slocum.

With a quick shake of his head, Slocum refused to take the star. He had worked on the wrong side of the law too much to ever put on a badge. It would make him feel like a hypocrite if he wore the badge and then found Jose Espalin and the hoard of Aztec treasure. He would not hesitate to gun down Espalin if the man got between him and the gold—and wearing a badge might slow him down the fraction of a second Espalin needed.

Slocum and the law had worked at cross-purposes too long for him to pretend he was a law-abiding citizen.

"Reckon I understand," Earhart said. Slocum wasn't sure if the lawman did or not. And it was a matter of no concern to him. Slocum had a back-shooter to find—and Aztec gold coins to load onto the rear of his sturdy sorrel.

"Get me some provisions," Slocum said. "And ammunition. I'm running low after a week and more of gunplay."

At this Earhart laughed. "Tularosa was a quiet place 'fore you rode in. Seems you were the trigger for a whole lot of killing and shooting."

"Not much has been my fault."

"None has been, Slocum. I know you're innocent of inciting any of the trouble. The entire town was about ready to come to a boil a month before you rode in. You happened by when it all exploded like a stick of rotted dynamite."

"Lucky me," Slocum said sarcastically. Earhart got ammunition and enough food to last Slocum a week from another man in the posse. Espalin had more than an hour's head start, and the rocky, sunbaked ground left little in the way of trail, but Slocum turned toward the Sacramento Mountains and guessed where the man was heading.

Pitalpitoque hunted for the gold Jose Espalin might already have found. Espalin would want to retrieve his find and get out of the region as quick as he could. That meant he'd make a beeline for the canyons where he could lose a posse and find his gold.

Without even acknowledging the sheriff's farewell, Slocum mounted and rode.

It had been both easy and hard these past six days. Slocum found Espalin's trail easily enough, but once the desperado reached the foothills of the Sacramentos, the path grew increasingly hard to follow. Only Slocum's well-honed skills kept him going until he overtook the man.

Now Slocum pressed his belly flat against hot rock as he peered down at Espalin squatting by a low cookfire. The mesquite wood rose in wispy gray-white curls and made Slocum want to sneeze. He held back the urge. Espalin had a six-gun at his side and two rifles with his saddle. It was hard to tell what the fugitive carried in his saddlebags. More gold? Slocum hoped so.

The sun worked its way behind the high rim of the canyon wall and brought sudden twilight to the area. Slocum shivered as the rock cooled under him as soon as the sun set. He was tired and had tracked Espalin for almost a week. He wasn't adapting as well to sudden temperature changes in the desert as he ought to. Even worse, Espalin started fixing dinner. The odors rising made Slocum's mouth water.

Working off the rock so he wouldn't dislodge as much as a single pebble, he slid down the back of the boulder. He pulled his six-shooter and took a deep breath. Then he went around and came up from behind. When he cocked the Colt, Espalin went for his own six-gun.

"You're dead if you try it, Espalin," Slocum said in a cold voice that matched the gathering chill. The desperado froze and turned slowly to see what danger he faced.

"You have hunted me down? Why?" asked Espalin. "Does the miserable life of McDonald mean so much to you? Of Walter Goode?"

"You killed them both." Slocum did not ask a question. He knew Espalin had done the crimes.

"Of course I killed them. McDonald was a fool and Walter wanted to stop the range war brewing."

"Why were you so eager to see the Stuarts and Goodes shoot it out?" This was the only reason Slocum could figure for the man's action.

Jose Espalin laughed harshly. "They kill each other, they neglect their cattle. I rustle them from under their noses, and they blame each other!"

"That's it? You wanted the cattlemen shooting it out so you could steal their livestock?" Slocum was amazed.

"A brilliant scheme!"

"Put your six-gun down. Over there. Real gentle-like," Slocum ordered, when he saw that Espalin was thinking it just might be possible to throw down on a man who had him covered.

Espalin did as he was told, then sank down to finish his dinner.

"This is very good. Would you like some?"

"I want information, not grub," Slocum said, moving to keep Espalin between him and the fire.

"I killed them both. What more do you want to know? I am proud of it!"

"You rode with Walter Goode. Everyone in town says you were partners."

"Partners have a way of getting on each other's nerves, no?" Espalin laughed harshly. "He was no longer useful to me. Did the sheriff believe he killed himself?"

"No," Slocum said.

"A pity. The man is more clever than I thought."

"You're stupider. You led me straight here," Slocum said.

"Where is here?"

"To the gold. To the source of these." Slocum reached into his pocket and pulled out one of the Aztec coins. He turned it over and over so it caught the light from the campfire.

"Beautiful coins, I think. But what do they have to do with me?"

Espalin was a bad liar. Slocum flipped the gold coin and let it spin in the firelight as he moved around.

"You found the Aztecs' gold. They're out here hunting for it."

"You work for them too? How many masters do you serve?"

"I serve myself," Slocum snapped. "Where's the gold?"

"Ah, you are not so unlike me. You are a thief who looks only to steal what is not yours." Espalin laughed. He stopped laughing when Slocum reached into his shirt and pulled out the green feather he had found. Espalin went pale as Slocum walked closer and showed him the peculiar plume.

"I know everything, Espalin," Slocum said. "You won't get far with the gold—unless we work together."

Slocum was bluffing. He implied he knew everything when he knew nothing. The Aztec gold was hidden, but had Espalin moved it? Was Pitalpitoque hunting futilely in the mine shaft, or was the treasure already on its way back to Tenochtitlán?

"You cannot know everything," Espalin said, but his eyes fixed on the peculiar feather. It rippled like silken green liquid in the faint breeze coming from farther up the canyon.

"You can't risk it," Slocum warned.

"What is it you are saying? A partnership between us? Why? Why would you need me if you know where the gold is, if you are in league with *it*?" The sheer loathing mixed with a touch of fear as he mouthed the word "it" rocked Slocum. Espalin was not as afraid of the cocked Colt Navy in Slocum's rock-steady hand as he was of the feather and what it stood for.

Slocum wished he knew what that meant.

He also wished he could pry out of Jose Espalin where the gold was hidden—and still find a way of getting the murderer back to Tularosa for the law to take its course. If Slocum had to choose between gold and justice, he would have to think on it a while. The lure of the Aztec treasure was great, but it burned like a knife in his gut when he thought about what Espalin had done to George McDonald and Walter Goode.

Neither had had a fair chance of defending himself. Espalin had cold-bloodedly murdered both men. Of that Slocum was as sure as anything in the world.

But the gold . . .

"So what are you to do?" asked Espalin. "Would you share with me the gold?"

Slocum didn't respond. In the distance he heard faint scraping noises, of leather moving lightly over rock. Or bare feet on the stony ground. He twisted and fired into shadow when he saw movement. The bullet ricocheted off dark rock, and then there was only silence.

"Espalin, get over here!" snapped Slocum. He turned back to the outlaw and found only emptiness between him and the campfire. If Jose Espalin had been a ghost, he could not have vanished any faster or more completely.

Slocum cursed under his breath. A single second of inattention and he had lost any chance of getting the hidden gold. Jumping over the fire, Slocum knelt and looked at the ground. Faint scuffs in the dirt led off into the darkness. Slocum listened hard to see if Espalin betrayed himself. He heard nothing now—not even the faint sounds he had heard before.

A small game trail wound between the rocks. Slocum raced along at a fast pace, oblivious to the possibility of Espalin laying a trap for him. When he didn't find the man after five minutes of hunting, he slowed and tried to settle himself. Headlong running into the night wasn't going to flush his quarry.

He dropped to his knees and looked at the ground. The darkness hindered him, but Slocum found where Espalin had come by recently. He followed the trail, alert for any place Espalin might leave to take to the high ground. Espalin kept moving along the trail—from the distance between footprints, at a dead run.

The game trail came to an open area dotted with a few scrub oaks and numerous low, dark shrubs where a dozen men might lie unseen waiting to gun down the unwary. Slocum disturbed a few animals milling about, and knew he had found a watering hole. More than this, the animals had not been disturbed by Espalin laying an ambush for him. Slocum went to the shallow pond, looking around constantly, and saw footprints in the mud along the edge.

He swallowed hard. Everything was explained now. The sound that had distracted him back at Espalin's camp. The reason he had fired and not hit anything. Where Espalin had gone. It was all revealed in a single clue at the pond.

Barefoot tracks, with Espalin's tracks in between, led off.

Slocum followed them a few yards until he saw how Espalin's toes started digging twin furrows in the dirt. He was being dragged along between two others.

Two barefoot Aztec warriors.

11

Slocum started after Espalin and his captors, then slowed and finally stopped. He remembered what Angelina had said about the Aztec chief and how he thought he carried the spirit of Montezuma's most capable general inside him, a ghost haunting a still-living human body. Such belief might make him crazy as a loon, in Slocum's mind, but it also made Pitalpitoque a very dangerous man.

He would think of traps and tactics and using his warriors the best way possible. Having lost a few already, Pitalpitoque would not risk any more unless it gained him his goal. By kidnapping Espalin, this meant only one thing: Pitalpitoque had not found the hidden gold.

"The son of a bitch *did* steal it," Slocum muttered, marveling at Espalin's audacity. His hand drifted to his vest pocket where the few gold coins rested, the one he had found on the road north and the others Jose Espalin had dropped when Slocum pursued him from the skirmish with Goode and the others.

Slocum squatted on his heels and thought hard about what to do. Blundering along in the dark wasn't the way to proceed. Slocum would only find himself captured and staked out alongside Espalin if he did. Slocum spat. He hated the idea he had to save Espalin.

Or did he?

How long would Espalin stand up under the Aztecs' torture? Slocum could follow them to where Espalin had hidden their gold, then steal it away before they could drag it back across the border and into Mexico. Then he sagged. He had no problem letting Pitalpitoque torture his captive, but Slocum realized stealing the Aztec treasure would never work. He faced a dozen or so warriors. They might be armed with nothing more than lances and bows and arrows, but they would be more vigilant than ever, knowing their gold had been stolen away once before.

Slocum wouldn't get the gold away from them; he would simply die trying.

Then there was Angelina. The lovely Aztec priestess kept pushing thoughts of the gold to one side, and this bothered Slocum. He shouldn't think with his balls. Gold would serve him far better for much longer, and he could use it anywhere he wanted.

Angelina was completely dedicated to retrieving the long-lost treasure for her own people, and would never be swayed from that. Lake Texcoco would turn golden with the reflection of so much wealth, and that would be fine with her.

Slocum rose from his contemplation and left the trail, finding a way through the tangled undergrowth that permitted passage with little sound. Now and then he snagged his shirt or drove a thorny limb into his face, but for the most part he felt safer, although the going was far slower.

The sixth sense that had kept Slocum alive through the war worked in his favor again. He didn't smell anything, he didn't hear or see anything out of the ordinary, but he felt a presence. Stopping, he tried to figure out what warned him. A faint darkness near the game trail he had abandoned was the only warning he had, and it was a faint one.

Then he saw the slight movement as the Aztec shifted position to ease his cramped legs. The warrior crouched where he could loose a feathered shaft square into anyone emerging from between two large rocks on the trail. If Slocum had passed through that gap in the rocks, he would have died.

His only question was whether another Aztec fighter guarded the far side of the gap. If so, killing this one might alert the other. But Slocum had to take the chance. If he left any Aztec behind him as he approached their main camp, he ran the risk of being attacked from two sides.

Slocum holstered his Colt Navy and drew his heavy knife. He moved like a light breeze through the small stand of trees and brush. At times he froze for long minutes. At others he moved only inches a minute. Then he sprang like a mountain lion. A quick slash of the knife ended the Aztec's life.

Slocum eased the man to the ground and quickly searched the body, finding nothing but a crude obsidian knife sheathed at the dead man's waist. He pulled the knife and thrust it into his own belt, not sure if it would be useful, but knowing it was wrong to leave behind any weapon he could carry easily.

Waiting a few more minutes convinced Slocum the Aztec was on lone sentry duty. Slocum returned to his off-trail path and continued, only to come back to the trail a few minutes later when he saw a small movement in shrubbery. He thought he'd missed the men in ambush, then saw the tight wire strung across the game trail. Anyone blundering into the wire would cause the bushes to shake and knock over stones precariously stacked.

"Camp's near," Slocum decided. Otherwise the small clicking of rocks as they fell would be swallowed by distance. He considered tipping the rocks and setting his own trap. Eliminating even another Aztec warrior would go a ways toward putting the odds in his favor, but he held back. Pitalpitoque's band would still outnumber him, and if their sentry or sentries did not return, it might set them all on his trail.

Slocum skirted the rock alarm and made his way out into a grassy area. Falling onto his belly, he worked his way forward until he got to the edge of the Aztecs' encampment.

He was glad he had not bulled his way in on Pitalpitoque. The Aztec chief had Jose Espalin staked out and was torturing him to learn the location of the gold, but the other prisoner posed even greater problems for Slocum. How was he to get the gold and then rescue Angelina?

The woman was securely bound with leather thongs to a pine tree. She struggled against the bonds and glared at Pitalpitoque and the other Aztecs, occasionally shouting something in a language Slocum did not recognize. Her words inflamed the two guards nearby and kept their attention focused on her. One poked at her with his feather-decorated war lance until she subsided. The way the two men exchanged lewd laughs told Slocum Angelina's star had set and she wasn't likely to be used well after the gold was recovered.

Slocum tried to figure how to get rid of the men without alerting any of the others, but the way Espalin was screaming distracted him.

He had to decide. Espalin or Angelina.

Slocum decided Jose Espalin could hold out a while longer. The outlaw was not inclined to give in easily, knowing once he did he was going to be killed and left for the buzzards. His only chance was to strike a deal with Pitalpitoque, something not likely to happen any time soon.

Pitalpitoque wanted the gold, and did not care how he retrieved it.

Moving in the darkness, Slocum circled the camp and camp up behind Angelina. He waited until the two guards turned from her to enjoy the spectacle of Espalin's torture. She started to taunt them again, but Slocum clamped his hand over her mouth.

"Hush," he whispered in her ear. "I'll get you free in a minute."

He used the captured obsidian knife to slice the woman's bonds, then thrust the sharp-edged weapon into her hand. He instantly regretted giving the fiery woman the knife. She surged to her feet and lunged forward, the blade sinking deeply into one warrior's back.

He let out a gasp and sank down, gurgling as blood gushed into his punctured lung. The other turned, startled at the sudden death visiting his friend. Slocum had no choice but to use his own knife. If he tried firing, he was sure to attract unwanted attention to the escape.

He stumbled as he lurched forward, his knife raking across the Aztec's chest. The man yelped as he turned, and hammered at Slocum with the butt of his war lance. The wood shaft glanced off Slocum's head and momentarily stunned him.

"You fiend!" cried Angelina. She whipped out the bloody knife from the dead man's back and used the point on the other guard. The tip entered just under his rib and surged upward to rupture his heart. He died with an outcry stillborn on his lips.

Angelina yanked the blade back, dropped to her knees,

and started to open the man's chest to rip out his heart. Slocum captured her wrist and pulled her away.

"Pitalpitoque," he warned. "He'll know what's going on if you take too much time."

"This one is dead anyway. I needed him to be alive," Angelina said with some venom.

"Too late to avoid trouble," Slocum said, dragging her behind him. Her naked breasts brushed across his arm and sent new tremors through his body, but urgency outraced any lust he might feel. Another guard had spotted them trying to make their getaway.

"I will—" Angelina started.

"Run," Slocum said, shoving her into the darkness. He dodged off at an angle to the path Angelina took. Slocum hoped to divert the guard's attention—and he did.

The Aztec warrior looked after Angelina, glanced in Slocum's direction, then chose to follow the woman. That spelled his death. The man lumbered after Angelina, and immediately found Slocum's arm circling his thick neck. Being tossed about like a rag doll, Slocum held on and squeezed tighter and tighter on the man's windpipe. The thrashing diminished, and finally died entirely.

Slocum hung on for a minute longer to be sure the warrior wasn't playing possum. Only when he was sure that all breathing had stopped did he release the man. Panting harshly, Slocum spun and started to draw. He wasn't sure if the others had heard and followed. He let out a sigh of relief when it looked as if Pitalpitoque was still occupied with torturing the information out of Espalin.

"John, John!" came Angelina's urgent call. "This way. We can get away from them!"

Slocum found her in the darkness and caught her up around the waist. She pressed close, and his heart was off to the races again. Angelina made quite an armful. He held her tightly for a moment, then pushed her away.

"We have to find a place to go to ground. When Pitalpitoque finds you're gone, he'll come hunting for you."

"He has no interest in me now. He thinks he is better than Quetzalcoatl. The fool cannot flout the gods! He will be punished for such heresy!"

"What caused the split in your ranks? You were helping him hunt for the gold."

"He thinks the one he tortures will tell him all he needs, that the gods are no longer needed to retrieve our treasure." Angelina spat like an angry cat. "He will keep the gold for himself. I know it! He will anger Quetzalcoatl and make—"

Slocum clamped his hand over her mouth again, pulling her down into the bushes. She fought only a moment, then heard what Slocum already had. The soft movement of bodies passed through the undergrowth. Then came others, hunting and not finding.

"We've got to get out of here. There's no way I can fight them all off," Slocum told the still-angry woman.

"*We* can kill them! They are traitors, heretics, and Pitalpitoque is worst of all!"

"Don't be a fool," he said. He wanted to shake some sense into her, but the noise that would create might mean both their deaths. Tipping his head in the direction of the canyon wall, he started off. It became increasingly less important to him if she followed. He wanted to get out with his head still fastened on his shoulders. He had killed three of Pitalpitoque's men, and Angelina had added a fourth to Quetzalcoatl's death roster.

"We can do it," she said, but her tone indicated she had come to the conclusion Slocum was right. She followed, grumbling under her breath. He wished she would fall silent.

He reached the canyon wall, then decided to do a little climbing. A faint path, possibly left by Apaches, lead to a rocky ledge twenty feet above the canyon floor. From this aerie Slocum knew he could spot Pitalpitoque or any of the Aztecs trying to sneak up on them.

And right now, he needed a few minutes of peace and quiet. He had been keyed up for far too long.

"Must we go there?" Angelina asked, seeing where he headed.

"I can hold off an army from there." He looked over his shoulder at her and felt his breath catch in his throat. She was about the most beautiful woman he had ever seen. Her running around naked to the waist like some dance hall whore bothered him, but he knew no one would ever confuse Angelina with the loose-moraled women. The haughty expression, the regal cant to her head, said that, clothed or not, Angelina was a princess, a priestess of surpassing power.

Her power began exerting itself on Slocum as he made his way up the rocky slope. He reached the ledge and fell flat, six-shooter in his hand. He watched carefully for some time to assure himself Pitalpitoque had not found their trail or seen where they had gone to ground.

"He won't find us," Slocum said. "He's got unfinished business with Jose Espalin."

"The gold," grumbled Angelina. "He will never stop until he has it for his own." She looked at him with her wide, dark eyes. "Do *you* know where it is, John Slocum?"

"Don't know," he said honestly. Then he added, even more honestly, "I wish I did. The secret is locked in Espalin's head."

"He will speak it then," Angelina said with grim finality. "Pitalpitoque knows ways of making a stone statue speak."

"There's nothing we can do but wait. Your former friend will expect us if we go traipsing back right now."

''He will not remain long. He will either pry loose the secret of the gold or he will take his prisoner, this Jose Espalin, and go elsewhere. He knows this camp is exposed.''

Slocum lay back on the ground, hands under his head. He stared up at the stars poking around the edge of the cliff above. Then he glanced over toward Angelina. She smiled a little and came to him.

''How are we to spend this time?'' she asked softly.

''Reckon we could get some sleep,'' he said.

''Ah, yes, sleep. It is important,'' she said, working to unfasten his gunbelt and unbutton his jeans. His hardened length came out and into her grasp. She stroked up and down it a few times, then applied her lips to the tip. Slocum gasped and wiggled about a little. This was good, but he knew what was better.

Angelina read his mind. She stroked a few more times and left a wet, parting kiss before stripping off her breechclout. Breasts bobbing gently, she straddled his waist. She positioned herself carefully, his meaty shaft directly under her, then sank down.

Slocum sank balls-deep into her heated interior. It felt as if he had been engulfed by a warm, clinging tidal wave that washed through his body. It crashed against his senses and made him even harder.

He reached up and cupped her breasts. They were firm and about a handful. He smiled. Anything more was a waste. And Angelina was about perfect.

His fingers caught the nut-brown pebbles of her nipples and tweaked. She sighed and then gasped as he began to work on both of the succulent mounds of brown flesh. His hands stroked over her smooth flesh, and came around to cup the twin globes of her ass cheeks. Kneading as if they were lumps of pliant dough, he got her moving up and down slowly, in a rhythm that sent tremors of desire lancing down into his loins.

"You make it so hard," he said.

"I noticed." She smiled broadly. Then she gasped as he began to squeeze on her rump, moving it around and causing different sensations to ripple through her.

"Not what I meant," he said. "Hard to keep from spending myself like a young buck getting laid for the first time," he said. Staring up at her made keeping himself under control all the harder. So lovely, so incredibly exotic, so undeniably sexy.

Angelina began moving up and down faster and faster now. Her groin ground into his, their most intimate flesh merging wetly. She gasped and moaned as she built up speed, then leaned forward so she could ram her hips down harder. When she did, he lifted off the rock and licked at a nearby nipple.

The woman gasped and arched her back. Slocum felt her inner muscles clamp down hard on him, as if she were milking him. The spasm passed and she began moving with more speed and deliberation now. A sucking sound filled the air, but Slocum doubted anyone would hear. He was more afraid of Angelina calling out in her passion.

Or him crying out.

He licked and sucked and teased at her nipples as she bent forward again. Their loins pounded together, Slocum lifting off the ground enough to meet her downward moves. Every impact pushed him that much closer to losing himself in her moist, clinging interior.

"Yes, John, oh, John, yes," she gasped out.

And then Slocum's hot tide rose and spilled forth. Angelina groaned and sobbed and tossed her head back, her long banner of lustrous midnight-black hair fluttering in the soft night breeze. Her body shook and shivered and responded to

Slocum's. Every muscle tensed, and then the delightful rictus passed all too quickly.

Then they sank down side by side, letting the stars light their faces and the puff of wind blowing down the canyon cool their bodies.

It was paradise. For a while.

12

"They've found us!" Angelina sat upright, but Slocum managed to grab and pull her back down to keep her out of sight. He listened hard and heard soft, indistinct noises, but nothing that told him an Aztec was sneaking up on them.

Rolling onto his belly, Slocum peered down the faint, rocky trail leading to their hiding place. A rabbit hopped along the path, stopped halfway up, and stuck its long-eared head straight in the air, nose working hard to find Angelina and Slocum. The rabbit peered around, decided it wasn't safe to explore any farther, and raced back down into the sparse stand of trees. Slocum let out a breath he hadn't even been aware he was holding.

"Your friends are off somewhere else. That wasn't anything to worry over." Slocum turned back to the woman. He caught his breath again, seeing her beauty. The morning sunlight gleamed on her naked body, turning it into fine bronze.

But no metal alloy was ever so soft and warm and pliant.

"They are not my friends," Angelina said bitterly. "They never were. I am their priestess, and they are now heretics following Pitalpitoque rather than the ways of righteousness."

"Powerful words," Slocum said.

"You should know." She turned dark eyes to him, as if to spear him. "You carry the feather of Quetzalcoatl. You have been chosen to do the feathered serpent's command."

"I found it. That doesn't mean I'm bound to do anything," Slocum said, pulling out the feather. It had remained unsullied by all the hard riding, the sweating, the hardships he had been through. It rippled like liquid as he moved it back and forth. Where the feather had come from he could not say, but he had never seen a feathered snake and wasn't likely to either. If he ever did, skinning it would give him a hell of a hatband.

"You are bound to him," Angelina said with finality. She reached out to touch the feather, stopping inches from it as if it might burn. Pulling back, she shuddered lightly. The movement held Slocum's complete attention.

How she could be naked like a whore or a savage, and yet seem so cultivated and even dignified, he couldn't say. She might have been some fancy lady sitting in the drawing room ready for afternoon tea for all the elegance about her. It was more attitude than clothing, that much was certain.

"I'm about out of ammunition, and what little food I have is in my saddlebags," Slocum said. He worried about his sorrel. The animal had been tethered near a patch of grass, but water would get to be a concern soon in the stifling heat trapped between the canyon walls.

"We go after Pitalpitoque," she said, as if not hearing him.

"I need something more than that obsidian knife," Slocum said. "If we fetch help, we can—"

"No! Others would be corrupted by the lure of gold, as Pitalpitoque has been. The coins must be returned to Tenochtitlán, as Quetzalcoatl has commanded!"

"Can't say I disagree with you," Slocum said slowly, knowing there wasn't a man in the posse hunting down John Goode who wouldn't turn around and go gold hunting if he showed them one of the Aztec coins in his pocket. Goode himself would abandon whatever war he waged against the Stuart brothers and their ranch hands if it meant more gold than a strong man could lift.

Slocum wasn't even certain Sheriff Earhart would be untouched by the pointing finger of greed.

He let out a short bark of a laugh. *He* wanted the gold and to hell with giving it to peasants in Mexico! They had never seen such wealth, and would never miss what they had never possessed. He could use the money wisely.

"Then we will go after Pitalpitoque," she said. "By now he must have forced the information from Jose Espalin."

"Espalin's dead," Slocum figured. "One way or the other, he is dead. I saw what they were doing to him. Even a man as cussed as Espalin couldn't stand what Pitalpitoque was doing to him, not for long."

"Then it is agreed." Angelina got to her feet and tried to go back down the trail. Slocum grabbed her arm and pulled her back to sit beside him.

"Don't go rushing off half-cocked," he said. "I need more ammo. And the way my belly's grumbling, food would be nice too."

"You are a warrior. Endure. And fight! We must go and stop Pitalpitoque before he steals the gold."

Slocum might have appreciated such single-minded behavior if it hadn't meant going without food—and having his Colt Navy's hammer drop on an empty chamber. One was an annoyance right now. The other might mean dying.

"We need supplies," he insisted. "And we need to make a plan. If we go running off in all directions, Pitalpitoque will snare us real easy."

"Not if we are careful. Quetzalcoatl is my god, and he will guide us. We go after Pitalpitoque. Or do I go alone?" Her challenge filled Slocum with a curious combination of anger and resignation. He knew she wasn't able to fight and win against the Aztec chief, but would try, with or without his help.

Anger that she wouldn't see how obvious it was to rearm before going on was quelled. He had a choice to make. Go with Angelina and keep her from getting caught again or abandon her.

"Let's go," Slocum said, "but I only have six shots left."

"And your knife and your strong arm and your quick thinking. You are well armed, John Slocum." She bent and gave him a quick kiss. In that instant he almost believed her. Almost.

Going back down the steep trail proved harder than going up. He slipped and slid and almost lost his balance more than once. Reaching the bottom of the trail, he saw their aerie was no longer safe from detection. The loose stones brought to the bottom of the trail pointed like an arrow straight up the side of the mountain.

He settled his six-gun and then checked his knife. Angelina clutched her obsidian-bladed knife and set off through the woods. Slocum trailed behind, every sense alert. It galled him, but he intended to let her spring a trap. He had to be close enough to get her free but far enough back not to get snared himself.

They reached the Aztec camp, and Slocum saw he had been right about Pitalpitoque not remaining there. The Indians had left soon after he had freed Angelina. The cold ashes in the campfire showed no new wood had been added overnight. He made a few quick sweeps around the perimeter, and found where the Aztecs had retreated.

"They went this way," Slocum said, walking slowly along the path. He saw something right away that struck him as odd. Bare feet were the rule among the Aztecs. One in the group wore boots. Slocum stood and looked around. "Where's Espalin's body?"

"I do not see it," Angelina said.

"He's with them then," Slocum said, dropping and letting the sun catch the distinct edges of the footprint. He didn't remember the pattern of the outlaw's boot, but who else could have made the track?

"Does this mean he has not spoken and Pitalpitoque thinks he can still get the information from him? Jose Espalin is stronger than I thought," Angelina said.

"Reckon so," Slocum answered, "unless he's cut a deal of some kind. Maybe he thinks he will get some of the gold and be released if he shows Pitalpitoque where the gold is hidden."

Angelina gave the response Slocum might have. She snorted in contempt at such maudlin thinking. If Espalin thought to form any alliance with the Aztec chief, he was wrong. Dead wrong.

They set off at a lope, covering the distance easily as they followed the trail left by the retreating Aztec band. Slocum saw the spoor was hours old, and had little fear he would run into a trap until they got closer to the warriors.

By midday he was sweating, thirsty, hungry, and beginning to think they would fall off the edge of the world before they overtook the Aztecs. He called to Angelina to stop.

"Rest," Slocum gasped out, wondering how she managed

to keep up such a pace without even appearing winded. "I need some water too."

"We must find them," she insisted.

"Rest first," Slocum said. He dropped to a log, wishing he wasn't putting so much distance between himself and his horse. He wouldn't be in any shape to fight if they found Pitalpitoque, in spite of Angelina's determination.

"We are not far from them. I can feel it!"

"We need water. And food," Slocum said. "I'll get some and—"

"Listen!"

Slocum stiffened, and his hand rested on the ebony butt of his six-shooter. Voices. He turned slowly, then frowned. The noise wasn't coming from the direction he anticipated.

"Someone else is out here," he decided. "That branching canyon, the broad, shallow one. May be riders."

"We must reach Pitalpitoque quickly!"

"All right," Slocum said, knowing that it might be Earhart and his posse approaching. Explaining to the sheriff wasn't in the cards. And the gold! Slocum wasn't going to share it with anyone.

Worse than that, if the posse blundered onto the Aztecs, they were likely to wipe out the Indians, and with them Jose Espalin. All chance of finding the gold would be lost.

Legs aching and his lungs heaving, Slocum ran along, matching Angelina's effortless stride. He tried to keep on the trail and watch for traps at the same time. He began to flag, and Angelina pulled ahead of him.

"Wait!" he called to her.

"Ahead," she whispered urgently. "They are ahead!"

Slocum rested his hands on his knees and bent over to catch his breath. With his pulse pounding hard in his temples, he couldn't hear a thing, but he took her at her word. Angelina was like a flea on a dog's back. Once she started chewing, she never stopped until she drew blood.

"We ought to circle and come at them from some other direction," Slocum said. "They'll be watching their back trail."

"That way," she said, pointing to their left. "I will go the other."

"Don't split up—" Slocum's words fell on emptiness. Angelina was already gone, not on the trail. He sucked in a few more quick breaths to steady himself, then headed in the direction opposite the one the Aztec woman had taken. Following her served no purpose if she was right about Pital-pitoque being somewhere ahead.

Slocum made his way through the tangled, thorny under-brush and peered past a pine tree into a grassy area. In the middle of the meadow stood Pitalpitoque and a half dozen of his warriors. They argued among themselves. Look as he might, Slocum could not spot Jose Espalin.

"The son of a bitch got away from them," Slocum decided. "How did you do it, Espalin?"

No easy answer came for that. If the Aztecs tracked the renegade, that made Slocum's chore even harder. He had to avoid the warriors *and* locate Espalin. Slocum slipped back and then stared up the tree. Like all pines, the limbs on this one started a ways up the trunk. Slocum began climbing, and finally got into the lower branches. The tree swayed and shook, but he kept climbing. He needed high ground to hunt for Espalin and to get an idea what Pitalpitoque intended to do next.

Through the needles he got a good view of the land between the tree and the edge of the canyon. No movement betrayed Espalin. And when Slocum tried to figure what the Aztec warriors intended, he was startled to find they had all vanished as if they were nothing more than mist in the hot desert sunlight.

He waited a few minutes, thinking they would show their hand.

Nothing. Slocum might have been alone. He didn't even see Angelina.

Cursing, he shinnied down the tree and landed heavily, going into a crouch. Slocum circled the clearing, and finally went to the middle of the meadow after finding nothing. He found the spot where the Aztec chief had spoken with his warriors, but nothing more. No evidence that Espalin traveled with them could be unearthed.

Slocum spun, trying to decide where to head next. He took off for the far side of the grassy expanse and could not find any trace of warriors, Espalin, or Angelina.

He took off his hat and smacked it against his leg. Dust rose in a cloud, then settled. Slocum had lost everyone.

13

"They didn't go past me," Slocum said to himself, working through all the possibilities. He looked longingly back down the canyon in the direction of his horse. The sorrel had been left far too long, and Slocum was getting edgy. More than this, his feet were sore from all the walking that morning. He needed to find a pool of water to soak his feet and ease the pain, but getting to one posed problems.

"I'll lose the tracks if I take too much time," Slocum grumbled. Following Angelina would not be easy, but getting after Pitalpitoque and the others might gain him a pile of gold coins. Unless Espalin got to the gold first.

"Who do I find first?" Slocum wanted Angelina, but she didn't know where the gold was. Pitalpitoque and the warriors accompanying him wanted the same thing, the gold, but Slocum knew his attention had to focus on Espalin. If the man had not yet revealed the hiding place where he had stashed the gold weeks ago, Espalin was still the key to a lot of Slocum's problems.

"Too bad Angelina doesn't have the gold," he said, turning back up the canyon to hunt for the path taken by the Aztecs. "I could find both things I want without wasted effort."

He hunted, but could not find any spoor. Pitalpitoque moved like the very wind, and Angelina wasn't any less capable. Whether they wanted to hide their trails or simply hurried on and left no trace, Slocum didn't care. The result was the same. He dropped to the ground and put his ear to a sunbaked patch of dirt to listen for footsteps. This didn't work well and wouldn't give him a sense of direction, but it was his only chance to detect the presence of the Aztecs.

He jerked upright when he heard distant pounding. Putting his ear back to the ground, he listened harder. He snorted in disgust. The sounds did not come from a human foot hitting the ground, even running. Slocum heard horses' hooves.

The gentle valley branching off to the right gave Slocum his first hint of approaching riders. He considered hiding, then realized they had spotted him and rode directly for him. His hand rested on the butt of his six-shooter, and then he relaxed.

Seeing who came up caused Slocum to curse nonetheless. Sheriff Earhart rode at the head of his posse. Slocum recognized many in the posse. Oliver Lee, Perry Altman, others he remembered from the earlier posse all accompanied the lawman.

"What you doin' on foot, Slocum?" asked Earhart. "You get your horse shot out from under you?"

"Left it down the canyon a ways," Slocum said, not wanting to explain his motives to the sheriff.

"Who you after?"

"Who are you after, Sheriff?" Slocum glanced at the others and saw they all wore makeshift badges on their vests. Earhart had turned out half of Tularosa to hunt for someone, and Slocum guessed it had to be John Goode. If it had been anyone else, there would be some representation from the Goode clan.

"Been up to my ears in a powerful lot of trouble, Slocum," Earhart answered. "John Goode upped and killed Charley Dawson. Have to bring him in for murder."

"And other crimes against the local folks," Slocum added sourly. This produced a few whispered comments about him from the Stuart faction. He didn't make any friends and had passed caring. He wanted to find Espalin and get the gold.

If he couldn't get the gold, he wanted to find Angelina. She might want someone to escort her back to Lake Texcoco and her precious city of Tenochtitlán. Slocum wouldn't mind a sojourn down south, not after all the trouble he'd put up with so far.

In no way did Sheriff Earhart and his lynch mob figure in Slocum's future.

"You haven't seen Goode, now have you, Slocum?" Earhart fixed him with a hard stare.

"Haven't seen hide nor hair of him," Slocum said. "I'm still tracking down Jose Espalin."

"Want him, and that's for sure, but Goode is getting everyone riled," Earhart said. "Should never have killed Charley Dawson over any danged woman."

"What happened?" Slocum asked, thinking this was the best way of getting the posse to move on. Let Earhart give him what he wanted to jaw about. Then he would continue hunting Goode.

"Goode killed Charley over Charley's wife. They was foolin' around, and Charley caught them."

Slocum wondered if Dawson had cared about McDonald being killed or if he had simply been objecting to Goode seeing his wife. Whatever the reason, Goode had gunned down someone the citizens of Tularosa must have thought highly of. Slocum smiled wryly at the thought that these men might be objecting to the loss of a woman many of them were seeing.

"Pity," Slocum allowed. "But John Goode's not out here. Not that I've seen."

"You catch sight of Espalin? Maybe the two varmints are traveling together, thinking to avoid the law," Earhart said. "Espalin was partners with his son, after all."

"Don't think so, Sheriff," Slocum said. That would be real irony. Espalin kills Goode's son and then Goode befriends him by getting him away from the Aztecs. No matter what kind of snake John Goode was, he'd better not turn his back on Jose Espalin.

"How close is Espalin, if you're tracking him on foot?"

"He might have gotten away from me. I lost the trail entirely," Slocum said honestly.

"Then maybe we ought to work together on this so's to kill two birds with one stone. There's a powerful lot of explaining Espalin has to do. John Goode can sing along with him."

"I need to fetch my horse," Slocum said.

"Oliver, you give Slocum a ride back down to wherever he left his mount?"

"All right, Sheriff, as long as you don't catch Goode without me." Oliver Lee's hand brushed lightly over the butt of the six-gun he had thrust into his belt where he could get at it quickly. Goode had less than a snowball in Hell's chance of ever standing trial with this bloodthirsty posse. No matter how upright Earhart was in maintaining the law, he rode with a bunch of wild men bent on vengeance for real and imagined crimes.

Perry Altman alone would put a bullet through the man's

head the instant he sighted him. Any friend of McDonald's would try to outdraw Altman for the honor. And Slocum had no idea what the other men thought of Charley Dawson being gunned down. Even if it had been a fair fight, the notion Goode had been messing with another man's woman struck these upstanding ranchers as criminal.

Hanging criminal.

"Come on up, Slocum," Lee said, reaching down. Slocum took the man's hand and jumped behind him. The horse shied under the weight, then staggered a few steps before adjusting. "This way?" Lee asked, pointing back in the direction of the Aztecs' camp.

"Go," Slocum said. They started off. He glanced over his shoulder and saw Earhart was taking a rest in the meadow. This bothered him because it meant the sheriff would wait for them to return. Slocum had no chance to slip away once he retrieved his sorrel without attracting too much attention.

"What you really been up to, Slocum? You vanished and nobody saw you for a week or more."

"Thought I'd get out of Tularosa and on the road for Santa Fe," Slocum said. "Espalin burned at my gut, though, until I had to find him or spend my nights worrying over it."

Oliver Lee nodded, as if this explained everything. Slocum wondered how long it would be until everyone in Tularosa knew about Pitalpitoque, Angelina, and the Aztec gold.

Slocum knew greed would override vengeance if they caught wind of a fortune hidden out here in the mountains. He fell silent and let Lee ramble on endlessly about everything that had happened in Tularosa and how lucky they were that their womenfolk were off in El Paso, though he worried about them, especially his niece. Slocum remembered Lee's niece had been engaged to George McDonald, but the tangled threads began to confuse and bore him.

"There's your horse," Lee said, half standing in the stirrups and peering through the trees. "You have the only rested horse from the look of her."

The sorrel had eaten well but needed water. Slocum knew they would have to find a watering hole somewhere. He needed the water as much as the horse. Fumbling around in the saddlebags confirmed what he already knew. He needed ammunition.

"You got any spare powder and slugs?"

"Not for your Colt," Lee said. "Maybe someone in the posse has some they can loan you. We'll need all the fire-power we can muster when we find Goode. He doesn't go anywhere without an arsenal."

Slocum got some jerky from the saddlebags and gnawed on it as they rode back to join Earhart and the posse. As they neared, the sheriff got the men back into the saddle.

"Sent the men out on foot to scout, like you were doing. Found a trail over yonder," Earhart said. He pointed toward the far side of the canyon.

"Espalin might be trying to get to the rim," Slocum said, shielding his eyes and studying the rocky cliff face. He worried that he would spot Pitalpitoque and the other warriors working their way up to get away with the gold. Seeing the half-naked Aztec warriors would set off Earhart to capture them and ask questions Slocum preferred were never asked.

His worries didn't bedevil him for long. Nowhere did he see even a dark dot of a bird circling in the cloudless blue sky stretching from rim to rocky rim.

"Might be," Earhart said. "Might be he is meeting up with Goode. They could have a secret place to get together."

"Why would Goode stay in the area after all he's done?" asked Slocum. "He has to know Perry Altman is still alive. He has to know Dawson is dead. Goode is no fool."

"He's an arrogant son of a bitch," said Oliver Lee. "He doesn't think we can do anything to him. He's flaunting his wealth, thinking he can buy his way out of any crime.''

''That so?'' asked Slocum.

Earhart shrugged. ''Reckon it might be. The circuit judge is a Texan and might have been the one who convinced Goode to move here. Can't believe Judge Carroon would intentionally fix a trial, but these currents run deep.''

''The judge and Goode were in the damned Reb army together,'' Altman said. ''I heard someone say that.''

''Don't go spreading rumors, Perry. It's not necessary. I know what he did to you, and that's bad enough. Don't think to make him seem any worse,'' chided Earhart. In a milder voice, he added, ''We'll catch him. I promise.''

A ripple of anger passed through the posse, and Slocum knew he was riding on a powder keg with a lighted fuse. How long before the keg exploded he could not predict. He had to be long gone before then—and with the gold coins.

''Don't know exactly what trail we're following, Sheriff,'' came the scout's shout from ahead. ''Looks like a bunch of Indians. Barefoot. Never saw an Apache go barefoot in country like this. They are always fixin' up their moccasins.''

''Barefoot?'' Earhart dropped to the ground and looked at a clear print in the dust. ''It's fresh. See the sharp outlines? It wouldn't keep like that more than a few minutes.''

Sheriff Earhart looked up and tried to penetrate the stand of scrub oak and pine ahead. Then he began to look up, toward the canyon rim. Two dark outlines showed.

''Up there, men!'' shouted Earhart. ''Might be Espalin and Goode trying to get away.''

A roar of anger rose from the posse. Rifles came out and lead started flying. Slocum shook his head. The range was too great for any hope of winging either of the climbers. And strangely, the two tried to draw fire. This alerted Slocum to a trap.

He knew they had to be Pitalpitoque's men—and they were acting as bait.

"Sheriff, don't go rushing headlong into this. It might be a trap."

"How can it be a trap? There's two men, we're hunting for two men. After them!" the sheriff ordered.

The ragged volleys ceased as the posse mounted and tore off into the woods, eager to catch the two men climbing to the rim.

Slocum felt Oliver Lee's hot eyes on him. To hang back now might mean he would hang later as an accomplice.

"What are you waiting for?" Slocum shouted to Lee. He put his heels to the sorrel's flanks and raced off after the rest of the posse. It might be a trap laid by Pitalpitoque, but Slocum had no choice but to ride into it. Anything less would put his neck into a noose.

Slocum ducked as a low limb flashed by his face. Bent low, he tried to keep the horse from running wild. He slowed a mite and let Lee thunder up next to him. They were some distance from the rest of the posse, but Lee didn't press it. He kept close to Slocum, as if thinking this might reveal their quarry. Slocum knew he had fallen out of favor with the people of Tularosa.

John Goode had no reason to take a liking to him, though they had never met. Jose Espalin would put a bullet between his eyes. And now the friends of George McDonald were growing leery of him because he wasn't as focused on catching Goode as they were. Slocum wasn't about to spill his guts about the Aztec gold.

He had the cold feeling in his gut that the posse would find out soon enough what trouble lay ahead.

He only hoped Angelina wasn't caught up in the middle of it.

Shifting his weight, he steered the horse away from Lee,

hoping to lose the man. Oliver Lee followed. And then from ahead came a horrendous crashing sound that drew both Slocum and Lee.

"What's going on?" Lee demanded.

Slocum didn't bother answering. He tried to pick his way through the trees so that he could find out what happened without exposing himself needlessly. A crunching, grinding sound was quickly followed by another loud crash of rock hitting the ground. With the sound this time came the frightened neighing of horses, men cursing loudly, and even a few random shots.

Bursting from the forest onto a rocky stretch that led to the canyon wall, Slocum took it all in with a single glance. Parts of the cliff had been pried loose and brought down on top of the posse. Slocum saw two men partially pinned under rocks. One struggled and bellowed for help. The other lay still. From the puddle of blood around him, the man had been crushed to death instantly.

"Up there, above us, fire on him! I know it's Goode! Get him!" Perry Altman danced around on the ground, waving his six-shooter wildly. He began shooting at the men higher up on the cliff face. At this range, hitting anything with a six-gun was a fool's pursuit. Slocum worried more about Altman hitting one of the posse—or him.

"Perry, stop it!" shouted Lee, the same thought going through his mind that had already passed through Slocum's. "You're going to make it worse!"

"Goode's getting away!"

"It's not him," Slocum shouted. "Those are Indians. Look at them!"

Altman stared at the men climbing above and hesitated. This gave Lee enough time to grab the gun away from his friend.

"Apaches, those are Apaches!" cried Lee.

"They aren't! That's John Goode!" Perry Altman fought with Lee to get his six-shooter back.

Slocum was more interested in what Pitalpitoque and his Aztec warriors were up to. They had reached the rim and vanished over the top. He doubted they were simply running for their lives. It had taken a few minutes to find the right boulders to push down on Earhart's posse.

"The whole damn cliff's coming down!" Slocum shouted. "Get back! Get away!"

The air filled with dust and rock heavy enough to crush every last man in the posse.

14

More rock tumbled through the air, smashing down with the explosion of a dozen sticks of dynamite. Slocum did not take his own advice to run away from the wall. He put his heels to his sorrel's flanks and bolted toward the canyon wall so the rock would fall past him. The horse's eyes showed white all around and its nostrils flared with fear, but Slocum kept control.

"Go on, go on!" Slocum kept his horse moving through the dust and destruction, ignored the moans and cries of outrage from the rest of the posse, and finally found a small island of safety pressed hard against the base of the cliff.

More rock tumbled from above, and then came a deathly silence. For the span of a dozen heartbeats, Slocum heard nothing. The dust obscured his vision, and he saw nothing. His nose wrinkled from the powdery dust, and he sneezed. This set off a rising protest from the surviving members of the posse. Through it all came the bantam rooster of a sheriff's booming voice.

"Dang it, get yourselves to safety. Don't let 'em mash you flatter 'n bugs! Move, damn your eyes, move, move, move!"

Slocum used his bandanna to wipe the dust from his eyes and blew his nose. By the time the wind carried away the cloaking, choking clouds to reveal the sheriff, Slocum had recovered enough to crane his neck around and peer up the towering cliff.

How Pitalpitoque and his warriors had scaled that rock face was beyond him. There were handholds here and there, but they had scampered up like flies. He tried to catch sight of any of the Aztecs and failed. Riding out a few yards, he stared up again, and thought he caught sight of a man dressed in a bright green feathered headdress. For just a moment the warrior peered down and then was gone.

"What was that?" wondered Oliver Lee, standing next to Slocum.

"What are you talking about?"

"Thought I saw a big green bird or something weird up there." Lee wiped the grit from his eyes. "Must have been one of Goode's boys. Nothing else likely to be up there."

"What about them Apaches we tracked this far?" asked Perry Altman. The man led his limping horse over. "Never seen them leave footprints like that, but times might be hard. Drought is killing off deer and they might be going barefoot."

"Nothing human is likely to have scaled that canyon wall," Slocum pointed out. "Not unless they have glue on their hands and climb like a monkey."

"Saw a monkey once in a traveling circus," Altman said, eyes slowly working up the rocky expanse. "Dangedest thing I ever seen. The keeper swore we was all relatives, the monkey and me." He laughed harshly. "If Goode made it up *there* without somebody on top pulling him up on a rope," he said, his fingers stabbing hard at the rim, "then I just might be a monkey's uncle."

"You won't get any argument on that," Sheriff Earhart said, hobbling over. His pants leg was bloody from a long gash in his right thigh. The sheriff shifted his six-shooter so it rode on his left hip so as not to chafe the wound.

"Looks like the posse is in poor condition to keep after Goode," Slocum observed. He was the only one who had not suffered some injury, either to body or horse.

"Reckon this ought to put steel into our resolve to find that no-account murderer," Earhart said. "I'm not willing to let Goode get away with this. How'd it look if we rode back into Tularosa without John Goode—and looking like this?" He waved his hands like a windmill to indicate the others. His agitation mounted. It was the first time Slocum had seen the sheriff this upset.

A few muttered about this, then resolve hardened, and Perry Altman led a cheer for the sheriff.

"We're with you," Altman cried. "We'll ride them bastards down to the ends of the earth!"

"We're almost there," Slocum muttered.

"We can't follow them to the top of the cliff," Earhart said. "Any of you know this country good enough to tell how to get up there?"

"At the end of the canyon," said a young man, hardly eighteen or nineteen, "there's a narrow path what goes all the way to the top. Apache trail, I reckon."

"Lead the way, Seth," Sheriff Earhart said. "Just don't get too far ahead."

"I'll scout with him," Slocum said.

"You do that," Earhart said, casting a cold eye on Slocum. The way the posse treated him had changed, Slocum noticed. It might be high time for him to simply leave when he got out of sight of the riders.

He and Seth rode briskly off in the direction Slocum had been traveling before the posse found him. Keeping a sharp eye out, he saw spoor the boy missed entirely. Drops of fresh blood, broken limbs, signs of struggle. He wanted to take a better look at the spoor, but Seth was eager to get to the trail and ride down on John Goode—or the men he thought rode with Goode. Slocum wondered if Seth would believe that they were chasing Aztecs bent on retrieving the treasure of Montezuma II for their god Quetzalcoatl.

He shook his head and smiled wryly. The boy would never believe that. Hell, nobody in the posse would.

Throw in a gorgeous half-naked priestess and a chief who thought he was carrying the ghost of a general dead for centuries around inside his head, and Slocum knew he would find himself locked up in some insane asylum before he could click his heels.

"Why you ridin' so slow, Slocum?" asked Seth. "The way's clear. All them Goodes are up yonder." He jerked his thumb in the direction of the canyon rim.

"Something wrong with my horse's leg. Seems to limp a mite."

"Didn't notice."

"You're not riding her," Slocum snapped. He slid from the saddle and pretended to study the sorrel's shoe for a stone. Seth circled restlessly, his attention fixed on the far end of the canyon. Slocum took the time to stare at a low blackberry bush. Bits of cloth had been ripped from a shirt. Slocum couldn't rightly remember, but the pieces might have come from Jose Espalin's shirt.

Espalin had struggled and left pieces of cloth behind. In addition, there were specks of blood in the dry dust. He had come this way, fighting as he went. But who was he battling?

Slocum had not heard gunshots, but he had to admit he had been busy with Earhart and Pitalpitoque and tons of rock being dumped on his head.

Slocum frowned as he reconsidered. Why did he think Espalin was armed? There might not have been any gunshots to hear. Angelina had the obsidian knife he had taken from a dead Aztec warrior, but none of the Indians had carried pistols or rifles.

"You coming, Slocum?"

"Shoe is loose," Slocum lied. He mounted and settled down in the saddle. Seth headed in the direction Slocum would have taken, so he rode along. It might come down to drygulching the boy to continue on his way, but Slocum hoped it would not come to that. Any slip would brand him as a Goode supporter.

"It's less than a mile. We can make it if we gallop," Seth said.

"My horse would throw the shoe if I tried. You go on ahead," Slocum said. He lost the trail he followed. Espalin might have slipped off to one side to go to ground. The renegade rustler and murderer might be only a few yards away, laughing at Slocum. He wished he could check an arroyo cutting through the rocky terrain, but Seth would have none of it.

"You want to wait up for the sheriff?" the boy asked. "He told us to go after Goode. You have a reason for hanging back? You haven't thrown in with those skunks, now have you, Slocum?"

"Goode tried to kill me when I first got to town. Ask McDonald about that," Slocum said, then caught his tongue. "Reckon you can't do that since he's dead. But the sheriff knows I don't have any love for John Goode or his kith and kin."

"You're not eager enough to string him up for my taste," said Seth.

"Sorry I don't share your need for a lynching," Slocum said. "I'd rather catch him and see he got a trial."

"A trial!" snorted the youth. "There's no way he'd ever get a fair trial that'd find him guilty. The judge is his good buddy."

"Might be," Slocum said. "I've seen worse in my day. I've seen judges who sold out to the highest bidder, no matter the crime. Weren't even honest crooks who stayed bought. They would change sides the minute they caught a hint of more bribe money."

"What you goin' on about?" Seth swung around in the saddle and pointed ahead. "That there's the trail head. You want to go on up first, Slocum?"

"We should wait for the sheriff," Slocum decided. "Might be a good idea to keep a few of the posse down here with rifles to cover us in case Goode follows the rim and decides to dump more boulders down on our heads."

"You have a real yellow streak in you, Slocum."

Slocum stiffened. This wet-behind-the-ears boy had never seen a fraction of what Slocum had endured without so much as a blink of an eye. Men blown into bloody mist by cannon fire, minie balls ripping off arms and legs, hangings where the condemned men's heads popped right off their shoulders—Slocum had seen all this and more and had never flinched.

Riding up a narrow, rocky path with Aztec Indians threatening to drop rocks on his head hardly counted after all he had been through.

"If you were a man, you would be dead on the ground right now. As is, since you're nothing but a boy, you can apologize. Apologize or back up your words."

Slocum shifted slightly. His hand rested lightly on his right leg, ready to go for the ebony butt of his Colt in its cross-draw holster. The coldness of his gaze caused Seth to back down.

"No need to get your dander up, Mr. Slocum. I didn't mean nothin' by it."

"Ask for my pardon or go for that hogleg you have tucked in your belt."

"I'm real sorry I said anything to annoy you. I didn't mean you was a coward or nothin'."

"Apology accepted." Slocum glanced over his shoulder and saw the lead element of the posse coming along the trail they had just covered. Straggling along behind the two riders came the sheriff and Perry Altman. And in a few minutes the entire posse had gathered around, Oliver Lee the last of the posse to arrive.

"Once we get to the ridge, where do we head?" asked Earhart. "You been up there before, haven't you, Seth?"

"I have," the boy said sullenly. He looked out of the corner of his eye at Slocum. If looks could kill, Slocum knew he would have a knife through the heart. And it hardly mattered. The boy had been taught a lesson about shooting off his mouth. A man backed up his words or knew enough to hold his tongue. A boy—or a coward—backed down.

Slocum knew he hadn't won any allies so far.

As the sheriff and the others discussed what to do, his mind wandered back to the blood and torn cloth on the bramble bush. Espalin had come this way. Slocum doubted he had gone up this particular trail, but there had to be other paths leading out of the canyon. Or maybe Espalin had penetrated deeper. If he was badly wounded, he might not be able to climb.

And what of Angelina? She had taken off like a scalded dog, going after Espalin. Maybe it was *her* blood. At this, Slocum shook his head and knew it wasn't likely. She was a fighter. The blood belonged to Jose Espalin, probably drawn by the sharp glassy edge of the priestess's obsidian knife or by Pitalpitoque's diabolical torture.

"It's a mighty dry ride back to Tularosa from there, Sheriff," Seth was saying when Slocum's attention returned. "It's closer to the Stuart ranch than it is to Goode's spread too."

"Where's the varmint likely to run?" Earhart spoke aloud but with the distant quality of a man thinking out loud. "How far does this canyon run?" he asked, changing the direction of his thought abruptly.

"Well, I don't rightly know that since I always went over to the Stuart brothers' ranch when I came this way," Seth said. "Might be a box canyon, or it might let out into some crossing canyon. The Sacramentos are filled with canyons nobody's traveled in years and years. Maybe never, 'less you count them danged Apaches."

"Always a good tale to be told about lost gold mines up here," said Perry Altman with a chuckle. "If I had a double eagle for every one of those I've heard, I'd be rich."

"You'd be dead. John Goode would have robbed you, then slit your throat," Oliver Lee said with bitterness.

"You mean we might get on over to the Goode ranch if we keep on along the canyon floor?" asked Slocum.

"You thinkin' he went to ground at his own place? That's plumb foolish, Slocum," said Oliver Lee. "Not even Goode is dumb enough to hole up on his own property. That'd be the first place the law would look."

"Was it?" Slocum asked of the sheriff.

"He took off running after he cut down Charley Dawson and came this way straightaway. There wasn't any chance for him to get on back to his own ranch. What are you trying to say, Slocum?" Earhart thrust out his chin in a belligerent manner, as if feeling his integrity was being questioned.

"Who knows the area better, you or Goode?"

"This is close to his spread. He probably has explored all this country at one time or another," Earhart admitted. "I haven't had reason to ever ride this way, but the others have. They know this country like the backs of their hands."

Slocum considered how easy it might have been for John Goode to give the posse the slip. They rode hell-bent for vengeance and paid little attention to the signs along the trail. Not a single man with Earhart had mentioned seeing the bloody trail or the bits of shirt caught on the blackberry bush. If Goode had let the posse ride past a hiding place or if he had found a different trail through the mountains, he could be anywhere.

Even back at his own ranch surrounded by his family, friends, and cowboys.

"Just thought you would check out the ranch house first," Slocum said. "If you had him in your sights the whole way, nobody can fault you for chasing him down."

Earhart's teeth ground together, but he did not press the point. He ordered three of the men onto the trail.

"You go with them, Slocum. Lead the way up. We'll cover you till you reach the rim."

Slocum nodded and wheeled his sorrel about. He knew when to argue and when to follow orders. Seth, Perry Altman, and another man from the posse rode behind him as he started up the narrow trail. The going got too steep to ride after only two switchbacks. Slocum carefully dismounted and led his horse.

"What's wrong, Slocum? You gettin' cold feet?" Seth called, emboldened by the presence of the other two men. "Heights make you queasy in the belly?"

"You and me need to talk when we get to the top," Slocum said in a level voice more frightening than if he had shouted at the boy. Seth subsided, looking around to be sure

Altman and the other man were there to back him up. Slocum didn't care if he took on all three. No one pushed him the way the loudmouthed boy was doing.

Halfway up the face of the cliff, Slocum stopped for a rest. The other three trailed behind. Sixty feet below he saw the sheriff and the rest of the posse sitting in a half circle, rolling smokes and taking it easy. Not a one studied the rim above for movement. Slocum stepped to the edge of the trail and tried to peer upward, and found a large rock outcropping prevented it. Pitalpitoque and his warriors might be pushing a boulder onto his head and the sheriff would never notice.

"You holdin' up the parade again, Slocum?" called Seth.

"I was wondering about the others joining the posse," Slocum said. From a quarter mile up the canyon came a half-dozen riders. And then he knew these were not joining Earhart. Rifle barrels glinted in the bright sunlight. Puffs of white smoke from the muzzles appeared an instant before the sharp reports reached Slocum.

"They're firing on Earhart!" Slocum cried. And then he stopped worrying about Earhart and the posse. He found himself in a world of trouble.

The riders turned their rifles upward and sent a hail of lead ricocheting off the rocks all around Slocum. Plastered on the front of the cliff, Slocum was a sitting duck to the sharp-shooters down below.

15

The first round sang off rock high over Slocum's head. Then the snipers got the range. Slocum fought to keep his horse from rearing on the narrow path—and failed.

"No!" he cried as the sorrel turned sideways and then lost footing to tumble over the ledge. Slocum's first reaction was to foolishly hold the reins, to stop the horse's fall through strength of his arms. The brutal tug yanked the reins from his grip and saved him from following the doomed horse over the side.

He watched in sick fascination as the horse bounced once off the cliff face and then plunged a last twenty feet to the ground. The sorrel kicked once and then died. Slocum got to his feet and almost lost his head. A bullet ripped through the brim of his Stetson, knocking it from his head. Again instinct came into play.

He grabbed for his flying hat. This time the motion saved

him. He stumbled and fell as another bullet tore through the space where his head had been a fraction of a second earlier.

"Damn them! They're potshotting us like birds on a fence!" cried Perry Altman.

"Get back down the path," Slocum ordered. "We can't make it to the top!" He heard Seth say something about leading them into a trap, but Slocum was too busy staying alive to worry his head over this. He drew his six-shooter and snapped off a couple of rounds. The distant riders were not threatened by the puny reach of his Colt Navy. They abandoned their long-range attack on those high above them on the trail, and turned their rifle fire toward Sheriff Earhart and the more immediate danger posed by the still-milling posse.

The earlier fight with the Aztecs had drained the posse of any reserve and had sorely wounded many of them. Shooting it out with John Goode and his family wasn't in the cards now.

Slocum watched Earhart try to whip the posse into shape so they could return fire. It never happened. They scattered and ran the best they could, some on foot and others galloping off in clouds of choking dust. Earhart went to ground, finding a place in the rocky foothills to shoot back at Goode. The renegade rancher waved his rifle in the sheriff's direction and shouted something Slocum couldn't make out, no doubt profane. Then Goode and those riding with him wheeled around and hightailed it.

"They're runnin'!" cried Seth. "The sheriff done drove 'em off!"

Slocum shook his head. The truth was as plain as the nose on his face. Goode might have slaughtered everyone but had chosen not to do so. The sheriff had made a brave stand, but nothing he had done had deterred Goode one iota.

The rancher had left because it suited him, not because he was afraid of the lawman or his posse.

The three behind Slocum on the trail got their horses turned around and headed back to the canyon floor. Slocum was a ways behind, and came up as Seth was telling Sheriff Earhart, "He signaled them, I tell you! That's why he wanted to get on to the top."

Seth turned and shot a hot look at Slocum, then swung into the saddle and galloped away a hundred yards before stopping. Slocum stared at the youth, knowing trouble when he saw it.

"He's got it in for you, Slocum," the sheriff told him.

"Nothing I haven't figured out already." Slocum brushed dust from his clothing and ran a finger through the new hole in the brim of his hat. "Reckon I can use a ride back to town. Let me fetch my saddlebags."

In silence he walked to where his sorrel lay. He made sure she wasn't still suffering, then dragged his gear off the dead horse. Slinging his saddle over one shoulder, he looped the saddlebags over his other arm. If he had to walk to Tularosa carrying this gear it might take a week.

"I can take part of it," Perry Altman volunteered. Slocum heaved his saddle behind the other man. Altman looked uneasy at lending a helping hand, and rode off without another word.

"Climb on behind me, Slocum," offered the sheriff. "It'll be a spell 'fore we get back to Tularosa, and that's something I'm not looking forward to." The small man heaved a sigh that shook his entire body. "We're returning like whipped curs, tails between our legs. And all because of a no-account Texan!"

Slocum had to put up with the sheriff grumbling until they reached Tularosa. Then the fat fell into the fire.

•   •   •

"Never seen anything lookin' like this before. You sure it's good?" asked the stable owner as he held up one of the gold coins Slocum carried in his pocket. The man peered at it as if it were paper and he could see through it. Then he flipped it a few times before dropping it on a wood plank nearby. He listened to the golden ring, satisfying himself it was genuine.

Slocum checked the shoes on the gelding he had bought with all but one of the Aztec coins—he still carried the one that had gotten him embroiled in the Tularosa range war safely in his shirt pocket. The others Jose Espalin had dropped had bought a decent three-year-old horse to replace the sturdy sorrel now lying as buzzard bait back in the Sacramento Mountains.

"They're good. Mexican pesos," Slocum said, knowing how far from the truth this really was.

"Seen pesos before. These ain't them."

Slocum shrugged. "Gold's gold, and you're getting paid five of the coins for the gelding."

"You're stealin' away a family member, you are," the man said insincerely, picking his teeth with a splinter from the plank where the gold coin had spun so delightfully. "Ride 'im in good health and be sure to treat 'im with respect."

"Thanks," Slocum said dryly. He was starting to run a tad low on money and needed to replenish his supplies. The only question burning at him was his destination.

Santa Fe or into the hills again to find Angelina and the gold? He had gone through hell and felt the gold was his reward for the hard times. And truth to tell, he missed Angelina as he worried more and more about her. She was so determined to retrieve the gold, she ignored the danger from Pitalpitoque and Espalin and now the rampaging John

Goode. Armed only with a volcanic-glass knife, she didn't stand much of a chance against any of them.

Looking for a poker game to build his poke, Slocum pushed through the doors into a tumbledown saloon at the edge of town, not a dozen paces away from the stables. He brushed off the horseflies as he went to the bar and ordered a shot of whiskey.

The barkeep said nothing as he eyed him strangely. Slocum thought nothing of it until he overheard four men farther down the bar arguing loudly.

"It's all Altman's fault Goode is being hunted down like a dog," a burly man with crisscross scars on his face declared in a drunken voice. "McDonald's friends are railroadin' him, I tell you!"

"Might be," said another, with a low-slung gun resting at his hip. Slocum had seen the man's like before. He looked and talked like a gunman, but would back down if it came to real shooting—or would drygulch anyone crossing him. "It's all a plot by the Stuart brothers to get John out of the territory."

"Get him out?" bellowed a third. "They want to *hang* the poor bastard! They can't get by with doin' that, though. John's got family and enough friends to keep 'em from doin' anything illegal."

"McDonald dyin'," mused the fourth, "all that might be a trick. We never saw the body."

"I did," Slocum said, wondering why he butted in. "McDonald was shot in the back."

"Who are you?"

"That's Slocum. He rode with the sheriff when they lit out after John," said the barkeep.

"You were with them when they found Walter's body too, weren't you?" The would-be gunman turned and rested his hand on the buckle of his gunbelt, as if he readied for a quick draw. Slocum ignored him.

"I asked a question," the man said in a more strident voice. Slocum knew when a man worked himself up into a lather.

"I found the body." He let the answer hang for a moment, then added, "He was murdered, just like McDonald."

"You sayin' the same man did both crimes?" asked the burly drunk.

Slocum shrugged. He had made a mistake coming in, and an even bigger one rising to the challenge offered by the quartet. He finished his drink, nodded in the foursome's direction, then left. A prickly feeling ran up and down his spine as he walked out of the saloon, wondering if the back-shooter of a gunman might decide to add another notch to his six-shooter's handle.

He reached the hot, dusty Tularosa street without being weighed down by an extra ounce of lead ripping through his spine.

It was time for him to move on, but he lingered a spell, his belly grumbling for food that didn't have maggots in it. It took less than a half hour for him to get a decent meal at a small cafe in the middle of town. Finishing the first meal he hadn't fixed himself in a week, he picked his teeth, left the small adobe building, and started down the street toward a general store, then paused when he heard Oliver Lee calling to him from another gin mill down a side street.

"Slocum, get on over here. We got to celebrate!"

"Celebrate what?" Slocum asked. They had been ambushed and lost one of the posse, the survivors needing the drunken town doctor to patch them up. He had lost the best horse he'd slung a leg over in years. To top it all off, they had not arrested Goode. Instead, he had ambushed them and gotten away with it. Slocum saw nothing to be happy about.

"Come on over."

Slocum glanced behind him to be sure the Goode faction had not liquored themselves up enough to follow him into the street, then headed for the saloon where Lee stood, wobbling slightly. No one in Tularosa seemed sober. That worried Slocum more than it ought to have. When the booze flowed, the bullets flew. He had seen it before and would see it again.

Too soon he would see it again, he feared.

"Buy you a drink, then I've got to get on my way," Slocum said, climbing the steps to the boardwalk. Oliver Lee's attitude changed visibly as Slocum neared. The man wasn't celebrating—not at all. Slocum had the gut feeling he was walking into a trap.

Inside the saloon stood most of the posse, including Perry Altman. The man's face was a dark mask, rage building by the minute.

"What's got you all so riled?" Slocum asked, knowing he would regret the answer. He shifted slightly so his right arm was away from the others. He could throw down and not have to move the muzzle of his Colt very far. With a spot of luck and a good bit of skill he might be able to drop three or four of the drunken cowboys before they reacted to cut him down where he stood.

It was long past time for Slocum to get out of Tularosa.

"You, Slocum," called Seth. The youth pushed through the tight knot of cowboys and belligerently strode toward Slocum. "You been tellin' lies to Goode's boys, and we don't cotton to it. Not at all."

"You have a problem with me, you tell me. Don't go spreading lies on your own," Slocum said coldly.

Seth looked left and right to reassure himself he had enough firepower to back him up before continuing.

"You told those owlhoots over at the Destiny Dance Hall

that Perry Altman killed Walter Goode. The word got back to us real quick.''

Slocum frowned. He had hardly left the other saloon, and didn't even recollect the name, and was being called out already because of an offhand remark. There had to be a telegraph between the two saloons.

''Never said that. Said the same person killed George McDonald and Walter Goode. We know what Altman was doing when McDonald was killed.'' He looked past Seth to Perry Altman. The man ran his hands over his arms, legs, and torso, remembering how Goode had tortured him on the bluff overlooking the road past Tularosa. ''We know what he was doing unless you're saying Altman lied about it all and is in cahoots with Goode. You saying something like that, Seth?''

''Don't go twisting this all around, Slocum. You're slicker 'n ary a greased pig the way you get out of trouble. We won't tolerate it anymore.''

''What you boys doing out here when you ought to be licking your wounds and getting ready to go back after Goode?'' came Sheriff Earhart's sharp question.

''He's thrown in with them, Sheriff,'' insisted Seth.

''You got a wild hair up your ass, don't you, Seth? If you pitched in against Goode, that snake wouldn't still be wigglin' around out there.'' Earhart walked over to the taller youth and butted up against him. Seth backed down, looking over Earhart's shoulder at Slocum.

''Don't think this gets you out of anything, Slocum. We know what you're up to, and we don't like it!''

Slocum was relieved to see all went back to their drinking. The sheriff swung around and came over to Slocum.

''And you, Slocum, you been shootin' off your mouth. I don't like that one bit.''

''Me? Shooting off my mouth?'' Slocum laughed harshly.

He was closemouthed most times, and had been reluctant to even talk to the four men in the other saloon.

"Doesn't seem like you, I admit, but word gets around town like wildfire. You're doing nothing but pouring kerosene onto the fire, and it won't go out that way, not when dynamite's been tossed in too."

Slocum saw the men in this barroom were knocking back drinks and whipping themselves up into a fighting frenzy.

"Been trying to leave Tularosa but something always catches me up," Slocum said, obliquely accusing Earhart of keeping him around. "It's time for me to push on."

"Don't get on back into the mountains, Slocum," Earhart said. "The posse's going after John Goode, and this time there'll be enough of us with enough firepower to make the arrest."

"Be sure to take along enough rope for Goode and everyone with him," Slocum said.

"That's uncalled for, Slocum," Earhart said, a knife edge to his words. "I won't let them sneak around the law."

"Good luck to you then," Slocum said, "because you're going to need it, Sheriff."

Slocum left the small man grinding his teeth together in rage. Getting the lawman mad at him wasn't too smart, but Slocum had been pushed too far too often. This wasn't his fight, yet he found himself in the center of it time and again. He couldn't care less about McDonald and Walter Goode getting themselves murdered—except that Jose Espalin knew where the Aztec treasure was.

Finding the elusive Espalin before Earhart got his posse rounded up again ranked high for Slocum. Too many unknowns remained for Slocum to simply up and leave. The trail of blood might have sprung from Espalin's veins—or Angelina's. Not knowing worried at Slocum like a burr under a saddle blanket.

"Find Angelina, find the gold, get the hell out of the territory," Slocum said, heading for a store. He spent a half hour inside getting his supplies, enough for two weeks. The bulk of his supplies turned out to be powder and bullets for his Colt and cartridges for his Winchester.

Slocum returned to the stable and loaded his saddlebags with his victuals and ammo. The gelding was getting used to him as he adjusted his saddle cinches and led the animal into the hot sun.

Slocum gathered the reins and started to swing into the saddle, ready to be quit of Tularosa once and for all, when an emotion-charged voice called his name.

"I'm talking to you, Slocum. You can't just turn your back and ride out, not after all them lies you told about me!"

"Seth's been putting strange notions into your head, Altman," Slocum replied. He considered mounting, then changed his mind when he saw how Perry Altman stood with his hand poised over the butt of his six-gun. He was a wound-up spring ready to explode, and it hardly mattered what direction he went. He was as likely to shoot Slocum out of the saddle as he was to turn and walk off.

"I talked to others. They're all sayin' the same thing, that you tole them *I* killed Walter Goode. They're startin' to say I ought to be strung up."

"They're all Goode's friends. What else do you think they would say?" Slocum tried to guess if Altman had worked himself up into a lather frothy enough to draw or if common sense would work. From the way he slurred his words, more rotgut had passed his lips going in than horse sense ever would coming out.

Drawing on the man would be the same as murder, but Slocum saw little choice.

"You're the one responsible for my woes, Slocum. I got to put it right. I got to!"

Slocum stepped away from his new horse, hoping Altman's wild shot wouldn't hit the gelding. And it would be a wild shot because Slocum's slug would already have ripped through his heart before Perry Altman's finger squeezed down on his trigger.

16

"I thought you was with us, Slocum," Altman shouted. "I never thought you'd be the back-shootin', low-down sidewinder hunting for a way to do us in."

Slocum settled his nerves and prepared to draw. Logic meant nothing. He had said the same man killed both McDonald and Walter Goode. Everyone in Tularosa knew Perry Altman was being tortured by John Goode at the time of McDonald's death. Following the trail back meant Slocum had implicated someone other than Altman. Slocum *knew* Espalin had done the killing—the man had bragged about it.

Slocum also held his tongue when it came to denouncing Jose Espalin because the man had taken the Aztec coins. Only he could make Slocum a rich man. After all Slocum had been through, he figured he was owed something for his trouble. After he got the gold from Espalin, he didn't care what happened to the murdering son of a bitch.

"I'm gonna shoot you where you stand, Slocum. I—"

A shot rang out. Perry Altman stiffened, then fell forward, face in the dust. His hand had reached the butt of his six-shooter but had gone no farther. Slocum blinked, not sure what had happened. His own six-gun still rested in its holster. He had been ready to draw but had not. He took a step toward Altman, who moaned and wiggled around in the dust like the snake he had accused Slocum of being.

A second shot sang through the air, adding a new hole to the brim of his already battered Stetson. He twisted and drew but found no target. Whoever had ambushed Altman was too well hidden.

"What's going on down there?" came Sheriff Earhart's shrill voice. The small man bustled along, six-shooter drawn. "You shoot him, Slocum? I'll see you in jail for—" Earhart lurched and dropped to his knees when a third shot came down the narrow alley leading to the stable. Whoever was firing on them was using a rifle and hidden far across the street.

Slocum caught sight of a rifle barrel poking out a second-story window in a saloon. The range was too much for him to use his six-shooter. He started for the rifle in his saddle sheath, but his gelding reared and pawed the air frantically, forcing him to control the horse or be trampled. Another deadly shot rang out, the bullet missing Slocum by inches. Then there was only silence.

The horse calmed, the stable owner came from the back with a double-barreled shotgun ready for action, and a small group began gathering at the mouth of the alley.

"Get the doc," Slocum shouted. "Sheriff's been hit." He stooped beside Altman. The man twitched like a dog with a back broken. Slocum kicked the man's gun away, then added, "Altman's hit too."

Slocum knelt beside Earhart. The man had gone whiter

than a sheet, but his clear eyes showed he was still completely in possession of his faculties.

"You've made some powerful enemies, Slocum. They tried to drygulch you and hit me by mistake."

"They shot Altman in the back too." Slocum was shoved back against the adobe wall as a dozen six-shooters were leveled at him.

"Shot Perry in the back. The sheriff too!" Oliver Lee cried.

"No, no, it's wasn't Slocum. Check his six-gun. Hasn't been fired." Sheriff Earhart fought to sit up. His hand waved futilely in the air, but the gathered crowd paid little attention to the lawman's protests. Then Oliver Lee moved to check the sheriff's contestation.

"He might have reloaded," Lee said, seeing all six chambers carried charges.

"No time," said the stable owner. "I was out here too fast. Besides that, I seen a muzzle flash yonder, from the second story of the Broken Spur. That last bullet almost got Slocum."

"You mean somebody shot both Earhart and Perry in the back and also tried to shoot Slocum from ambush?" The question hung in the air.

"That's what I seen, and if any man among you says different, let me know right now." The hostler shoved out his chin and dared anyone to call him a liar.

"Maybe he's thrown in with Slocum," suggested Seth from the edge of the crowd.

"Get out of here, you snotty-nosed little worm!" shouted the stable owner. "You don't do nothin' but cause trouble. Run on back to your mama and tell her what a miserable liar her only son is!"

This set off minor fistfights in the crowd as they argued over what the hostler said. Slocum yanked his six-shooter from Oliver Lee's grip and shoved it back into its holster. The sheriff eyed him but said nothing. No matter what he said, Slocum knew he had run out of goodwill with Earhart and everyone else in Tularosa.

Not that he had ever wanted any.

"Here's the doctor," Slocum said, backing away. "Time for me to get the hell out of here."

"Who shot at you, Slocum?" asked the sheriff. "Who got me and Altman?"

Slocum shook his head. It might have been Seth or it could have been any of the men who had been in the saloon backing John Goode and his clan. For all that, he could have sold tickets and had a line around the block of men wanting to take a shot at him.

The only question Slocum had was one of accuracy. Had the sniper wanted to kill him or had he hit his real targets?

"Not as bad as you usually get, Earhart," the doctor said, seeming more sober than any time Slocum had seen him. "I'll see to Perry." The doctor pushed his way through the crowd and went to Altman's side. He fussed and ripped at the bloody shirt, and made Altman wince as it pulled free of the bullet wound. Even from over the doctor's shoulder Slocum saw Altman's wound wasn't serious. He had probably fainted when he was shot because of all the booze in him.

"Ride, Slocum, ride on out and don't come back to Tularosa," Sheriff Earhart said, holding his arm to keep it from flopping around.

"Nothing'd please me more," Slocum said, mounting. The gelding shifted nervously, not used to be surrounded by so many people. Slocum's unaccustomed weight also spooked the horse, but it settled down when he guided it through the crowd and into the dusty street.

Slocum couldn't help looking up into the window of the saloon where the bushwhacker had shot at him. He almost expected to see a rifle poke through the dingy curtains. Nothing happened.

He rode out of Tularosa slowly, aware of the townspeople all staring at him like he was a leper. Slocum brushed it off. He was glad to be away from this town. The more he had tried to help the sheriff and its citizens, the worse off he had become. It was time for him to concentrate on improving his own lot.

And that included putting Jose Espalin into a shallow grave. Espalin was the author of most of his woes, and for that Slocum wasn't the least bit forgiving.

As he rode north, his mind raced. He had a day or two before Earhart got up a new posse to go after John Goode. The man had to be dug out of his ranch house. To get there Earhart might ride up the same canyon where the posse had met with such disaster. Slocum had only a limited time to find the trail left by Espalin and follow it, avoiding Pitalpitoque and locating both the gold and Angelina.

"That's quite a tall order," he said to himself. The gelding turned its head and peered at him with a big brown eye, wondering about its new owner and the way he talked to himself. Then the horse settled down and lengthened its stride. Slocum appreciated the power in the animal. If it had half the heart his sorrel had possessed, they could ride to the ends of the earth and back.

He hadn't ridden a half hour down the road when he began to grow uneasy. The feeling someone was spying on him grew until Slocum could no longer deny it. The road dipped and rose through one arroyo after another. Rather than staying on the road, Slocum cut down a deep, dry riverbed and found a mesquite giving faint shade. He swung from the saddle and tethered the gelding to a thorny limb.

He took the opportunity to sample the tepid water in his canteen and to wait. It didn't take as long as he'd thought.

And his tracker was almost as much a surprise.

Almost.

Slocum rose from concealment and grabbed his Winchester from the saddle sheath. He swung back in the direction of the road and levered a round into the chamber, but John Goode had already spotted the place where Slocum had gone to ground.

The Texan might have had supernatural powers considering the quickness with which he spotted Slocum readying his rifle for a killing shot. Goode let out a yelp and dug his spurs into the flanks of his horse. The animal neighed loudly and jumped as if someone had stuffed a lighted stick of dynamite up its rump.

Slocum's shot went wide.

John Goode roared out a blue streak of curses, then vanished over the rise leading out of the arroyo. Slocum swung into the saddle and went after the man, wanting to have it out with him once and for all.

"I missed you in town, Slocum!" came the angry cry from beyond the sand dune. "I won't miss this time!"

"You shot Altman and the sheriff?" This brought Slocum up short. He knew no reason for Goode to carry a grudge against him. The others in town might all be gleefully sighted in and trigger-squeezed on, but why him?

"What you have against me?" Slocum called, looking around. He knew better than to go over the rise in the road. He would end up with a hole the size of a silver dollar in his chest if he did. "Ever since the first day I rode into Tularosa, you've been gunning for me. What have I done to you?"

"You and McDonald were in cahoots to steal my horses."

"Who told you that? I'd never met McDonald before the day you tried to blow him apart with your shotgun."

"Espalin wouldn't lie to me about this," Goode said. With

that single statement Slocum knew it all. Jose Espalin was at the center of a whirling dust storm, kicking up lies and stealing from every side. He had bragged about rustling cattle. Slocum didn't doubt he'd also stolen the horses Goode worried over.

Worst of all, it would do no good for Slocum to tell the aggrieved man any of this. His son was dead by the hand of the owlhoot he trusted most.

"Where's Espalin? You seen him lately?" Slocum asked, edging around the sand dune and hoping Goode had not anticipated his flanking action.

No answer meant John Goode was readying himself for the kill. Slocum rode around the dune at a gallop. The rancher hadn't had time to prepare a decent ambush. He jerked around, startled that Slocum had not appeared where expected.

Slocum got off three rounds before Goode fired back. The slug ripped past Slocum's head, but he kept on. He had to end this now or Goode would be on his trail forever—and all because of Espalin's lies.

Slocum fired again, and then the usually trustworthy Colt Navy jammed. Cursing, he bent low and tried to run Goode down. The tactic didn't work. Goode fired twice more, and the second slug left a shallow, painful crease along Slocum's arm.

As he jerked to the side involuntarily, the gelding lost its footing. Rider and horse crashed to the ground. Slocum was slower getting to his feet than the horse, which took off at a frightened gallop.

Slocum sat in the sand, gun jammed and his right arm burning as if he had shoved it into a smithy's forge. He waited for Goode to finish him off. The bullet never came.

Ignoring the pain, Slocum knocked open his Colt and pried loose the cylinder. He cleared it and snapped it back into the frame. He had only one shot, but that was all he needed.

He turned his attention from his six-shooter to John Goode, only to find the man had fled.

Slocum climbed to his feet and cautiously went to the spot where Goode had lain in wait. From the tracks in the sand, the man had scampered up and away. Listening hard, Slocum heard the pounding of hooves.

Goode had hightailed it.

"Is the gold worth it?" he asked himself, taking off his sweat-soaked bandanna to bandage the bloody groove along his right arm. "Is Angelina worth it?"

He spat grit and blood from his mouth as he went to track down his gelding. He hated to admit it but the answer to both questions was the same.

Slocum heaved a sigh. Tracking Goode had been a chore, but he had kept at it. Try as he might, the rancher wasn't skilled enough to shake Slocum. Doubling back, covering tracks with a creosote bush dragged behind his horse, crossing rocky patches, John Goode had done it all. And none of it worked.

Lifting his injured arm to keep it from going stiff, Slocum looked across the valley and saw Goode riding slowly into a stand of pines. The day was cool, finally, and a brief late summer rainstorm had kept it that way.

"You're getting careless," Slocum said, staring at the distant rider. Goode probably thought the rain had wiped out the last of his tracks. He considered galloping after Goode, then decided that wasn't the way to catch the rancher. Goode had shown too many times his penchant for sniping.

Perry Altman and Sheriff Earhart were testaments to that. And it would never do getting captured. Again, Perry Altman was a good reason. Goode was lower than a snake in the grass and more dangerous.

Skirting the broad valley added an hour to reaching the trees, but Slocum had no trouble finding Goode's tracks. Hoofprints in the muddy ground were better than a sign with an arrow pointing ahead. Alert for a trap, Slocum rode deeper into the trees, meandering back and forth but keeping Goode's trail in sight.

Slocum reined back when a shriek of pure agony echoed through the woods. It might have been bait for a trap, but Slocum doubted it. No one faked such pain.

The cry of distress came again, trailing off in a low moan. He tried to figure if it came from the direction taken by Goode or off to the left. As much as he hated to pass up capturing Goode—and probably gunning him down for all he had done—Slocum could not let anyone suffer. Another, weaker moan pulled him away from Goode's trail.

Dropping to the ground, Slocum tied up his horse and then advanced on foot. As he was coming to think his ears had played him false, he came across a small campfire. A branding iron sizzled in the flames, but the hand guiding the iron was nowhere to be seen.

The stench of burned flesh made Slocum's nose wrinkle. He circled, and finally saw Angelina staked out spread-eagle on the ground behind a fallen tree trunk. The hot iron had been used on her arms, leaving wicked wounds behind.

"Angelina!" he cried, not thinking. She turned her dark eyes in his direction and tried to call out. A gag in her mouth muffled the words.

Seeing it, and remembering the cries that had attracted him, sent Slocum's hand flashing for his Colt Navy.

Trap!

It closed instantly. A rope dropped over his shoulders. As he pulled out his six-shooter the lariat tightened and yanked him off his feet. Falling from a tree limb, hanging on to the other end of the rope that pulled Slocum off the ground to swing helplessly, was a grinning Jose Espalin.

17

"Look at what the cat dragged in," Espalin said, grinning broadly. It took all his skill to keep Slocum's feet just off the ground. Slocum swung back and forth, kicking hard, trying to get the rope off his upper arms. With his arms roped to his sides, he was as helpless as a newborn calf.

"Don't swing so much or you'll hurt yourself real bad, Slocum," Espalin warned. The man grunted as he hoisted Slocum another few feet off the ground, then fastened the end of the rope around the tree trunk to let Slocum spin slowly in the wind. "You look like a side of beef hung out to dry," Espalin crowed.

Slocum bit back a cry of pain as the lariat cut deeper into his flesh. His arms turned numb. Even if he could hold the six-gun he had dropped, his fingers would never work on the trigger.

"Yes, sir, you look real purty danglin' up there, Slocum.

Too bad the rope's not around your scrawny neck!'' Espalin laughed and came over. He cocked back his arm, made a fist, and waited so Slocum knew what was coming. Then Espalin unleashed a jab straight to Slocum's gut. Slocum braced himself the best he could, but the power of the punch still took away his breath. The second blow was a haymaker, coming around Espalin's body and landing smack in the middle of his belly.

The world turned black, and Slocum fought to keep from vomiting. A few more punches put him away.

Slocum wasn't sure how long he was out. The blackness crept away slowly, replaced by shooting pains in his gut. His arms had long since turned to wood. He turned slowly from where he was hanging, trying to find Espalin. If the outlaw got close enough, Slocum figured he could wrap his legs around the man's neck and try to bulldog him down.

It wasn't much of a plan, but it gave Slocum some hope.

"Where are you?" he called when he didn't see Espalin. He feared what the man might do next to Angelina. The branding iron and the burns on her arms showed Espalin was capable of any atrocity.

He had learned well from John Goode.

Or was it the other way around?

"Espalin!" Slocum shouted. "Where are you?"

A puff of evening breeze set him to spinning faster, giving him a full view of his surroundings. He saw nothing of Jose Espalin or Angelina. This pushed his anxiety up higher and higher. Then he got hold of his emotions and thought hard.

"Why's he left me alive?" Slocum wondered aloud. He could guess why Espalin had spared Angelina's life—this far. She was a beautiful woman and raping her would be only a lesser crime for a man like Espalin, hardly noticed in the midst of even worse ones.

After all, he had bragged about shooting McDonald in the

back, and had won Walter Goode's friendship before turning on him, murdering him, and sparking a range war. What crimes other than rustling had Espalin committed since blowing into Tularosa? Slocum wasn't sure he wanted to know.

Most important to him was getting free of the rope and settling the score he had with Espalin. Any other crime would be paid in the single report from a six-shooter.

Tensing and relaxing his shoulders as he wiggled did nothing to free the lasso. It was cutting into his flesh now, huge welts swelling up past the rope to hold him even more firmly. When he tried swinging to get closer to the tree trunk, he heard a loud cry—and this one wasn't ripped from Angelina's lips.

"You little bitch!" shouted Espalin. "I'll learn you good." Espalin came running past, pulling up his drawers and waving his six-gun around. He stopped in front of Slocum and sneered at his captive.

"You look real nice danglin' there, Slocum. Real good."

"She get away from you?"

"Can't get far. She's hobbled," he said. Espalin hitched up his pants, fastened the belt, then hefted the six-shooter as if considering what to do with it. Slocum held his breath as Espalin cocked the gun, then walked behind him.

"Go on, struggle, Slocum. I like to watch that," Espalin taunted. Then Slocum's head slammed forward as Espalin buffaloed him. The world turned red this time as blood rushed into his eyes. Then everything drifted away, no matter how Slocum fought to keep a grip on his consciousness.

When Slocum became aware of the world again, the first thing he noticed was the lack of pressure against his arms. The ropes no longer threatened to cut him in two straight through the shoulders. But when he tried to sit up, he couldn't. Blinking hard, he got a hint of what had happened.

"Yep, Slocum, you're right. I cut you down. Kept thinkin' on how resourceful you are. Get your legs around the tree trunk, shinny up a ways until the rope gets some slack, then you might just sneak away."

"I wouldn't do that," Slocum said earnestly. "I'd hunt you down and kill you. Then I'd leave your carcass out for the buzzards and coyotes, except it would make them puke."

"Thass what I like about you," Espalin said, walking around and peering down at the bound Slocum. "You're such a goddamn diplomatic soul!" Espalin kicked him in the ribs.

Slocum struggled to sit up. A second kick sent him tumbling backward into a rocky pit. He crashed down, barely avoiding landing headfirst. The fifteen-foot fall shook him. Espalin's voice sounded as if it came from a thousand miles away.

Craning his neck, Slocum looked up to where the man stood on the lip of the pit.

"What's the weather like down there, Slocum? It's lookin' like rain up here!" Espalin spat on him.

Slocum couldn't figure it out. Why did Espalin bother keeping him alive? To torture him, probably, but this was better than swinging back and forth from a tree limb. And there was no sign Espalin was going to use the branding iron on him as he had on Angelina.

Why was he still alive? Not knowing the answer gave Slocum a small measure of hope. If he could string Espalin along, he might get out of this predicament alive.

Then *Espalin* would be the one to rue the day.

Slocum worried at the ropes binding his wrists behind his back. Espalin had looped the rope around Slocum's waist and then fastened his wrists to that, making it awkward even to stand, much less work on the fetters.

"What are you planning to do, Espalin?" Slocum called up. "Talk me to death?"

"No, Slocum, I'm gonna be real nice to you—and to the Mexican bitch."

"She got away, didn't she? You figure on using me as bait to lure her back? Angelina is too smart for that."

Slocum doubted he meant squat to the Aztec priestess. She was dedicated to returning the gold to her people. That was all. Slocum could rot in the pit before she even noticed.

"She'll be back. Getting those hobbles off won't be easy. And then she's got a letch for you."

Slocum wished that had even a grain of truth to it. He knew better. Forcing his back against the rocky wall of the pit, he got his legs under him and stood. The square pit was hardly eight feet on a side. From the sloping side, Slocum guessed it had been blasted at some time in the past. Getting out would be a chore, even with his hands free. And with Espalin standing guard above, it would be impossible.

As soon as Slocum started dislodging rocks in the dirt sides of the pit, Espalin would be alerted.

His mind turned to other matters. Why had Espalin kept him alive? That gnawed at him like a rat with a fresh hunk of meat. The murderer had shown no mercy with McDonald or Walter Goode. Why did he hesitate now when Slocum was completely at his mercy?

"She'll come back, Espalin!" Slocum shouted. "She'll be back to cut out your heart!"

No response. Slocum walked around, trying to catch some sign of Espalin on the edge of the pit. He had blotted out the evening stars before. Now even this faint silhouette had vanished.

Try as he might Slocum could not get free of the ropes binding him. He changed tactics. One side of the pit sloped up steeply. He tried running at it, feet driving hard, toes digging into the dirt, in an attempt to get up and out of the pit. If Espalin had left, this might be his only chance of escaping.

The more he tried, the more tired he got. Slocum finally subsided and let himself slide down the loose dirt to the bottom of the pit. He considered other schemes for getting out of the pit, but with his hands tied, none looked promising. He dropped to a sitting position and began scraping his ropes back and forth over the sharpest-edged stone he could find.

Using his hands, he thought he might be able to scramble up far enough on the single sloping pit wall to get free. Then there would be hell to pay. Espalin would end up dangling from a tree—with the rope around his neck.

Slocum had broken a few strands when he heard shouts and curses in Spanish above him. Then came more intricate curses in a language he did not know.

"Angelina!"

He tried to move to break the woman's fall as Espalin tossed her into the pit. All Slocum succeeded in doing was getting his body under hers.

They crashed to the stony floor. Breath knocked out of him, Slocum lay gasping for a minute. Angelina kicked him several times as she got to her feet and shouted at Espalin.

She waved her fist in his direction, and received only a mocking laugh as a reply.

"Enjoy yourselves," Espalin said. "It just might be your very last night—ever!"

"Glad to see you're all right," Slocum said, panting harshly to get his wind back. The woman looked frazzled, and was covered with cuts and burns from her torture. But she seemed in better shape than he was in. Slocum kicked and got his feet under him again.

"Can you get me free? Together we might get out of here."

"Sorry, John Slocum, I am so sorry I got you into this." She worked for several minutes getting the ropes off. Slocum almost screamed as circulation returned to his hands. It felt as if a million burning needles were being thrust into his skin.

He massaged his wrists with numbed fingers.

"Let me do that," Angelina said. She came to him and began working her strong fingers over his wrists and forearms, stroking along his fingers and bringing the blood back. He felt blood pumping elsewhere too, but it seemed inappropriate considering their predicament. He tried to push his longing for her away.

It proved difficult because she was naked save for a thin loincloth that hung in tatters and hid nothing.

"Why hasn't he killed us?" Slocum asked. "He wants something, but there's nothing I have that can interest him. It's sure not squeamishness about murdering an unarmed man that's slowing Espalin down."

"He wants the gold," Angelina said.

"What? I thought he already had it."

"He fears Pitalpitoque," she said, stroking up and down his arms now. Slocum winced as she located the shallow wound on his right arm.

"So? If he has the gold and Pitalpitoque doesn't, what's to be scared of?" Slocum saw the expression change subtly on the woman's face. "Why am *I* still around? Even if he thought Pitalpitoque had the gold and could ransom you for it, I'm not needed."

"Pitalpitoque does not know where Espalin hid the gold. I know this."

"Espalin is scared of something. What is it?" Slocum thought he had guessed the answer, but it was too fantastic for him to believe.

"Quetzalcoatl. I am the feathered serpent warrior's priestess. Espalin wants me to call off his wrath so the gold can be taken away.''

"He's afraid of some ghost god?"

"Quetzalcoatl is real. You carry his feather." Her hand slid inside his tattered shirt and stroked over the long, silky green feather stashed there—and his chest. "You are chosen to do his bidding."

"What you're really saying is that I'm still alive to convince you to call off Quetzalcoatl?" Slocum laughed harshly. "He thinks you have power over this feathered serpent and that I have power over you?" He looked down into her dark eyes and asked softly, "Do I have any power over you?"

"Yes," she replied.

She kissed him hard. Slocum pulled her close and felt her naked breasts crush into his chest. Her strong leg circled his, and she rubbed herself up and down on his upper thigh, her intimate flesh turning slicker as her inner oils whispered out.

"We can't," he said. "We shouldn't. He might be watching."

"If he watches, we can never escape," she said. "And this truly might be our final night in this world. We must live it to the fullest."

Slocum glanced up, but saw nothing of Espalin. He reckoned the killer would be making lewd comments if he waited and watched. More likely, he was off getting some dinner. A rabbit for the stew pot would go mighty good, Slocum thought.

Then his mouth was filled with Angelina's kisses and her probing tongue and her needs. He shared those needs. And she was right. This might be their last night. The condemned might not get a last meal, but this could be better.

Slocum stroked over the woman's tangled black hair and pulled her face up so he could kiss the sweep of her throat. His mouth moved lower, to the deep canyon between her bare breasts. His tongue licked and teased and found just the right places atop each mound of flesh to stimulate her. She moaned and sobbed. This time she experienced pleasure, not pain.

Slocum wanted to make her forget the terrible scars she would have on her arms where Espalin had tortured her with the branding iron. He wanted her to forget Quetzalcoatl. He wanted her to forget everything but the joy he brought her.

His mouth worked down to the slight dome of her belly, and his hands cupped her firm, well-muscled rump. He pulled her down to her knees as he sat back on a low rock. She knelt in front of him and reached over to unbuckle his belt and unbutton his jeans. Slocum let out a sigh of relief as his erect manhood escaped its cloth prison.

Angelina took it firmly in the curl of her fingers and tugged gently, moving it toward her most intimate crevice. He gasped with need as the head of his manhood slipped along the dark-furred terrain between her thighs.

Then she lifted one leg, stepped over, and sat down on his lap. He sank fully into her yearning interior.

For a moment, they remained unmoving, locked silently in the pleasures flooding their bodies. He marveled at the way his aches and pains vanished, replaced by mounting desire. His arms circled Angelina's trim body and pulled her closer. Again her breasts mashed down against his chest. But this time she began moving, lifting slightly and dragging her hard nipples across him.

The movement proved even more potent lower down. He slid from her heated interior until only the thick head of his shaft remained within her nether lips. Then she dropped down, smashing hard and grinding her hips around, as if his cock was nothing more than a spoon in a mixing bowl.

She moved slowly, building their passions until Slocum could stand it no longer. His arms circled her waist and he stood. The woman's weight forced her down so even more of his length vanished within her.

"Oh, John Slocum, it is so good. You fill me so much!"

She curled one leg around his waist and he cupped her buttocks. He began lifting and dropping her body to simulate the rhythm as if he had her laid flat on her back and he moved between her legs.

Up and down, with greater authority, he moved her body until she was writhing with unstoppable desire. Her tightness around him crushed like a hand in a velvety glove. Angelina's leg around his waist tightened, pulling her even closer. Slocum began arching his back and then straightening. This produced an in-and-out movement that ignited the hidden passions in both of them.

Angelina let out a cry of stark desire. Her body trembled like a leaf in a high wind and clung passionately to him. The hidden muscles within clamped hard on him and drew forth his seed. He spent quickly, his own desires at a breaking point.

Sweating and breathless, they clung to one another for some minutes after. Then Slocum gently lowered her to the ground.

"If this is the last night, we've done well with it," he said.

"Can it be our death?" she asked. Then resolve hardened her sex-softened features. "No! Quetzalcoatl will never permit it!"

Slocum looked from Angelina to the top of the pit. It wouldn't be Quetzalcoatl that got them out of there. It would be their own efforts. He might have been foolish taking the time with Angelina, but he didn't think so.

He could attack the problem of escaping with renewed energy now that he had a reason. This *wasn't* going to be the last night he spent with Angelina. It *wasn't*!

18

Slocum wanted to kill something. He would start with Jose Espalin and go from there, but right now he had to focus his anger toward reaching the edge of the pit. The harder he tried to get up the slope at the north wall of the pit, the worse it crumbled. He had almost buried them both with his last try at running up it, grabbing and scrabbling and trying to get his fingers curled over the top of the pit.

Covered in dirt, he sat for a moment to catch his breath. He was no closer to getting out than when he started.

"Why'd they even dig this pit?" he wondered aloud.

"It looks like the start of a sacrificial well," Angelina said. "We might be the first to die here."

"I'm willing to switch places with Espalin," Slocum said, standing. He looked from the almost naked woman to the rim. He rubbed his hands on his jeans and said, "I can boost you up. If you get out, do you think you can find a way to avoid Espalin long enough to get me out?''

Slocum worried about this plan. He had no idea where Espalin was. Sitting at the small campfire eating? Sleeping? Had he slipped off to fetch the gold?

"I will cut out his heart!" she cried, duplicating a threat Slocum had made earlier. "His heart will be offered as sacrifice to my warrior god!"

"He's mine," Slocum said, keeping the anger down. "I want Espalin to know who's bringing him deliverance from his pathetic life."

"Then I should boost *you* out," she said, mocking him. Slocum considered this for a moment, then discarded it. Angelina was too short, and he was not certain she could give him enough of a boost to reach the top of the pit.

"If I boost you out, will you try to get me out?" he asked.

"Then I will rip his eyes out with my fingernails," she said solemnly. "I will break his arms and legs—but I will let you kill him."

"Don't need anything fancy to get out. Sneak around if you have to." Slocum bent and cupped his hands like a stirrup. Angelina put her foot in his hands. The sole of her foot felt like boot leather as he grunted and heaved, rocketing Angelina upward. Her fingers clawed wildly at the loose dirt at the edge of the pit.

For a heart-stopping second Slocum thought she was going to come tumbling back, but Angelina gained a foothold in the soft dirt as she scrambled up and over. He watched her vanish. They had produced a loud cascade of dirt and stone.

Then there was nothing. In the pit the usual night sounds were muffled. He heard nothing of Espalin—or Angelina. He wanted to call out, but knew better than to warn Espalin, should the man be keeping watch nearby. He might have fallen asleep, permitting Angelina to creep up on him.

As much as Slocum wanted to end Jose Espalin's miserable life, he resigned himself to accepting it if Angelina got there first to slit the man's throat from ear to ear. Dead was dead and Espalin would have gotten what he deserved.

It was just that Slocum wanted the pleasure of the kill.

He jumped a foot when a dark shape snaked through the air and crashed down against the pit wall.

"Climb, John Slocum, climb!" came Angelina's urgent order. "I do not know where he has gone, but he is not in camp!"

Grabbing the rope, Slocum began climbing. His battered body complained at the strain and his injured arm almost failed him, but he kept moving, feet kicking and climbing and his hands pulling. He crashed, waist-down, over the rim of the pit and then squirmed forward like a snake. He knew better than to silhouette himself, should Espalin be waiting in ambush. He trusted Angelina, but Jose Espalin was a conniving back-shooter and might have fooled her.

"You see?" she said, crouching by his campfire. The faint embers glowed but gave off little heat.

Slocum made a quick circuit of the camp, finding his trusty six-shooter tucked away in Espalin's gear. He felt better with it hanging at his left hip. Angelina had found a hunting knife and brandished it, as if every slash in the air ended in Espalin's gut.

"Where do you figure he went?" Slocum asked. He had not found any tracks leaving the camp.

"We must be close to the gold," Angelina said. "Perhaps he has gone to stand guard over it."

"Maybe Quetzalcoatl ate him."

"Do not joke, John Slocum. You are the feathered serpent's chosen one. Your duty will become clear."

"My duty's to avenge a couple deaths and a lot of trouble caused by Espalin," Slocum said. It would be better if the man stood trial after the sheriff arrested him, but Slocum was more interested in justice than following the letter of the law.

"Your duty is to return Montezuma's gold to his descendants. They need it!" Angelina said hotly.

Slocum didn't reply. He wanted that gold for his trouble. Before he could decide whether to argue the point with the woman, he found a broken bush. The limb pointed away from camp.

"Here's where he left camp. Fresh sap, branch hasn't snapped back. Espalin went this way less than an hour ago," Slocum said. Staying close to the ground, he found more traces. Tracking in the dark was difficult, and he dared not light a lucifer to check the spoor he found, but he was good. Damned good.

"What is in this direction?" asked Angelina, keeping close. Slocum shook his head. He had no idea what had lured Espalin away from his two captives. A man so superstitious as to need an Aztec priestess to protect him from a feathered serpent god before he retrieved gold he had stolen fair and square was bound to do things no reasonable galoot was likely to do.

Slocum motioned her to silence. The ground was chopped up. More feet than Espalin's had kicked up dust here. From his reading of the tracks, Slocum put together a picture of the trouble Espalin had walked into.

"He was ambushed. Looks like Pitalpitoque and his friends."

"Look!"

Slocum had his six-shooter out and cocked before he saw what Angelina had already seen. He lowered the six-gun and turned slowly, hunting for any sign of Pitalpitoque and his warriors.

Propped against a rock a dozen yards away sat Jose Espalin, head slumped and hands at his sides. An Aztec war lance had completely spitted him.

"Does this mean Pitalpitoque knows where the gold is or did they shoot first and regret it later?" wondered Slocum.

"Listen!" Angelina grabbed his arm and turned him in the direction of loud rattling of chains and clanking of wagon wheels. "Pitalpitoque has the gold and is moving it away!"

"There's that much?" Slocum asked, astounded. He had thought the hoard to be nothing more than a strongbox filled with gold. A wagon meant more gold than a dozen men could carry.

He'd be more than rich once he got the gold. A personal rail car, maybe a saloon of his own, a Mississippi riverboat, anything at all would be within his grasp—if he got the gold away from Pitalpitoque.

"I will cut his throat. He steals the gold," Angelina said angrily. "I know he violates our pact with Quetzalcoatl!"

"Are you sure he's stealing it rather than just taking it back without you? Maybe he wants the honor bringing back so much gold would give. Pitalpitoque might have considered you a rival for his command over his warriors."

"He steals the gold," she insisted.

Slocum passed Espalin's body and shuddered slightly. Another lance might be waiting for him. He could turn and leave, poorer for his misadventures but still alive.

"You *must* help," Angelina said, her fingers digging into his injured arm. Slocum tried not to flinch.

"I want to see what we're up against. There might be a way out of this. Pitalpitoque doesn't know we're anywhere nearby. With Espalin dead, he probably thinks no one can stop him."

Slocum set off, Angelina following. She clutched her knife as if intending to use it at any second. Slocum doubted the Aztecs had guards posted if they had discovered the gold's hiding place and needed every hand to load it.

More clanking and creaking from wagons on the move came from up the canyon. Slocum tried to remember if there were roads crisscrossing the area. Extensive mining had brought heavy equipment into the Sacramento Mountains ten years earlier. When the silver mines petered out, the miners had abandoned the mountains for richer, newer strikes over in Arizona. But the miners had also left behind roads.

"They might reach Tularosa along some deserted road," Slocum said. This made him laugh aloud. The sight of Pitalpitoque and his warriors riding into town in wagons sagging under the weight of gold would shake up Sheriff Earhart and both sides in the blood feud brewing there.

For a moment, Slocum's curiosity almost got the better of him. How would that fracas come out? Would Goode triumph or would the Stuart brothers and the people aligned with them run the Texans back where they came from?

He knew that really didn't matter. These feuds came and went constantly. He had no love for either side, though he wanted to put a bullet into John Goode for trying to bushwhack him. Slocum knew he couldn't settle the score with everyone in town.

"There, see?" Angelina brushed against Slocum, bringing him back to the real issue. Gold. Pitalpitoque and the Aztecs carting off their gold coin.

He saw two warriors struggling with the balky team of mules pulling a long-bed wagon. They didn't know squat about driving a team. That might be the only thing giving Slocum the chance to steal the gold away. Otherwise Pitalpitoque might have been long gone with every last grain of gold dust in the treasure trove.

"They cannot!" Angelina cried. Slocum grabbed her arm and swung her around, pulling her to cover.

"Not yet. We need to know if this is the only wagon. I

don't think so. How many men are left? Including Pitalpitoque?''

"I do not know," Angelina said. "It doesn't matter. I
will—''

"You'll get yourself killed and then what? Pitalpitoque
dances away with the gold." Slocum watched as the two
Aztecs fought the team down a double-rutted road, long since
overgrown with weeds. Following them would be easy. He
refused to charge forward and find himself in worse trouble
than being in a deep pit.

He smiled wryly. Being in the pit with Angelina hadn't
been all that bad, now that they were free of it and Jose
Espalin.

"I must stop him." Angelina clutched the knife in her
hand until her knuckles turned white. When Slocum heard
something new and different, he released her.

"Riders coming," he said, thinking fast. The only riders
likely to be out in the mountains were either Goode and his
henchmen or Sheriff Earhart and a posse. Neither could be
allowed to see the gold wagons or the Aztecs. Too many
questions could be answered with a single word: gold.

"What do we do?"

It pained Slocum, but he knew he had to do this. "Go
after Pitalpitoque, but be careful. I'll be along before you
know it. Watch where he goes. He can't get too far."

"What will you do until then, John Slocum?"

"I'm going to send whoever's riding down hard on us in
some other direction."

"You will do what is right. I know it!" Angelina kissed
him hard. As she pressed close, she reached into the front of
his shirt and grabbed the green feather. The woman raced
off, waving the feather high above her head and whooping
like an attacking Apache. Slocum started to go after her, to

quiet her, then saw the first of the riders. His hand clenched on the butt of his six-shooter.

"Seth!" Slocum called. "What trouble are you getting yourself into?"

"Slocum!" The youth reined back hard. "I might have known we'd find you out here. You helpin' that owlhoot get away?"

"You mean Jose Espalin?"

"Who else? He's a murderin'—"

Seth cut off his diatribe when Earhart and the rest of the posse rode into view. The youth glared at Slocum, considering how easy it might be to shoot him down without the sheriff seeing him. But the way Slocum stood, hand on his Colt Navy, made killing him impossible. Seth subsided, but anger seethed in his eyes.

"Slocum, you still around? You got a good reason?" demanded Earhart.

Slocum turned slowly, making sure Angelina was out of sight. The Aztec priestess had run off fast after the gold-laden wagons. And of Pitalpitoque and his men, there was no trace unless Earhart hunted for it. In the dark, seeing the weeds crushed down required some work.

Slocum knew Seth wasn't a good enough scout to notice on his own, and if he gave the lawman something to keep him busy, no one in the posse was likely to notice the recent passage of heavy wagons.

"Real good reason. I was after the man who killed both McDonald and Walter Goode," Slocum said, locking eyes with the sheriff. "I found him. He's back there." Slocum jerked his thumb in the direction of Espalin's body.

"You finish him off?"

"He—" Slocum stopped for a moment, then knew the answer. "Apaches got him. Don't know what he stumbled onto. A war party maybe."

"Haven't heard any rumbling about them, but they are around," Earhart said. "They pushed rocks on us before." He looked around nervously.

"I've scouted the area," Slocum said quickly. "No trace of them. I think Espalin has been dead for a spell."

"Figure they killed him, then moved on?" asked Earhart.

"He prob'ly killed Espalin himself," muttered Seth. Slocum considered doing something about the boy, then figured it would work out eventually. Seth would push the wrong man and bullets would fly. Slocum had no doubt about the outcome.

"Go see for yourself," Slocum said. "Back down the trail a ways." He set off, the sheriff and rest of the posse close behind. It took him a while to find Espalin's body, but when Earhart saw it the lawman turned to Seth.

"Go pull that damned lance out of his chest, boy."

"Why me, Sheriff?"

"Because I told you to!" roared Earhart. "Any fool can see Indians did this to Espalin."

"Justice has been served," suggested Slocum.

"He confessed to you?" asked the sheriff.

"Said he killed both George McDonald and Walter Goode," Slocum said. "That was the way I always figured it."

"That'll settle the dust a mite," Earhart said, watching as Seth angrily yanked the Aztec lance from Espalin's chest. "I got Goode in jail back in town."

"What are you out here for then?" Slocum had thought Earhart was hunting for Goode, but this sounded more serious.

"Goode's clan insisted we find Espalin. Facts kept piling up that he was the root of all the evil flowering in Tularosa," Earhart said. The sheriff heaved a sigh and took off his hat, wiping his forehead with his bandanna. "Suppose I ought to let Goode go free."

"He might not have killed McDonald, but he tortured Perry Altman," Slocum said. "And he had to be the one who winged you and shot at me. And hit Altman back at the stables."

"I know, and he gunned down Charley Dawson, but letting him go free will defuse a situation turning nastier by the day. If I let him make bail, folks might cool down a mite."

"What'll Altman say? What about the others?" Slocum looked significantly at Seth, as the boy flopped Espalin's corpse over and brushed away the bugs already eating the body.

"Altman doesn't need to know your suspicions about the stable shooting, now does he?" Earhart looked significantly at Slocum. "It's little enough for me to have a gimpy arm if it prevents more men dying."

"That's mighty big of you, Sheriff," Slocum said, meaning it. He had seen lawmen who would ride to the ends of the earth to avenge an insult. Earhart's wound counted far more than simple name-calling.

"Peace might be better served if you'd *really* get on the trail to Santa Fe," the sheriff said.

"When I get my horse, I'll be gone."

"Will you now?" Earhart said, cocking his head to one side. "I always had the gut feeling you were playing a different game. Just don't cross me—or anyone from Tularosa—again. Got that, Slocum?"

Slocum nodded. The sheriff helped Seth get Espalin's body slung over the back of the boy's horse. The rest of the posse turned and started back in the direction they had come. Finding Jose Espalin dead had ended this posse's ride.

When the others had gotten out of earshot, the lawman turned to Slocum, smiled wryly, and said, "As I said, I don't know what game you're playing, but I hope it works out for you.'' He turned and pointed to the lance. ''I know that's no Apache weapon.''

With that Earhart galloped off into the darkness, vanishing in seconds.

Slocum let out a breath he hadn't known he was holding, then went to find his horse. Rescuing Angelina from whatever trouble she had gotten into by now would require a fast horse for their escape.

19

Slocum was glad the sheriff had not insisted on looking Espalin's camp over. Slocum gathered the dead man's gear, figuring it might fetch a few dollars when he got somewhere he could sell it. He threw the gear over the back of Espalin's horse, then saddled his own. The gelding appeared glad to see him. Slocum counted this as a good sign the horse was accepting him. He hunted for something to give the horse, but couldn't find anything. The few lumps of sugar he usually carried in his saddlebags had been ground to powder.

"When we get to Socorro or somewhere farther north," Slocum promised the horse, "I'll see you get a bag of grain." He cast a final look around the campsite and then rode out at a canter, eager to find Angelina but not willing to take the road too fast, fearing the gelding might step in a gopher hole and break a leg.

Slocum rode steadily until dawn poked pink fingers above

the canyon rim. He began worrying. He ought to have over-taken the Aztecs and their gold-laden wagons by now. More to the point, he ought to have spotted Angelina.

Both Pitalpitoque and the Aztec priestess had vanished.

He slowed to be sure he was still on the right path. The occasional ruts in the road showed wagons had passed this way. He couldn't tell if *the* wagons had come this way, if he was following them, because of the sunbaked ground. As he rode, Slocum began to feel more and more exposed. Any-one in the undergrowth along the road or sitting atop the canyon rim could see him easily.

The cavalry had never figured out, after long years of be-ing ambushed, how the Apaches always knew their location. All the Indians had to do was go to the high ground and patiently wait. A dust cloud moving slowly was a dead give-away. Slocum didn't kick up quite as much dust with his horse and Espalin's trailing along behind, but it was enough for a keen-eyed Indian.

He didn't doubt for a second the Aztecs were as astute as the Apaches.

The sun poked up over rocky edges and shone down with searing heat. He considered waiting until the afternoon be-fore continuing, to get the sun out of his eyes, but caution was shouted down by his need to find Angelina. If she had been captured, her life might be measured in minutes.

And beyond this, Slocum doubted the Aztecs could have traveled this far with their gold so fast.

"Did I miss the trail or are they flying along, wheels barely touching the ground?" he asked his horse. The geld-ing snorted and shook its head. "So you figure the mules are finally pulling for all they are worth?"

Slocum considered this a moment. The Indians he had seen were far from being skilled mule skinners. This ought to have slowed them, not sped them along the road.

Even with the sun in his eyes, he decided to press on. Hardly had he gone a hundred yards when he came to the first wagon, overturned in a ravine next to the road. He listened hard and studied the brush ahead and saw nothing. He hopped from horseback and slid down the slope to the wagon. Its rear axle had broken, but Slocum doubted this was the reason the wagon had left the road. The harnesses were ripped and the mules had run off.

He edged around the wagon and saw immediately that the Aztecs who had driven it were gone. So was the gold.

He began searching for some sign of what had happened. Whatever had pushed the wagon from the road was something more than bad driving. There was no sign of the wagon actually rolling down the hillside. It was as if a gust of wind had picked up the wagon and lightly tossed it here.

"Tornado? Don't think so." Slocum had never heard of a twister forming in mountains. Over near Fort Sumner they spotted one now and then, but it was nothing like Kansas or even Texas.

A sudden glint caught his eye. He scooped up a single coin.

"It *was* carrying the gold," he said in triumph. But where the Aztecs had taken the gold, he couldn't tell. No footprints disturbed the dirt around the wagon. For all that, it seemed as if the wagon had been lying here for long seasons, wind and sun and rain weathering the ground around it.

Huffing and puffing, he made his way back to the road. He tucked away the solitary gold coin and started walking along the road, hunting for a sign to tell him what had happened. He found only the twin wagon wheel tracks of another wagon.

Already the hot, dry wind whipping along the canyon worked to erase the tracks. He hurried along, a coldness forming in his gut. He feared what he would find ahead. A quarter mile farther, he found a second wagon. Like the first, it was overturned and off the road, no hint of how it had come to be moved a dozen yards and then tipped over. Unlike the first, it had not rattled down a ravine.

"No tracks to or from it," Slocum said, puzzled. He put his hand to his six-shooter as he approached.

No Aztecs. No gold. Nothing.

Frowning, Slocum wondered if there might have been a third wagon. If so, it had to be moving danged slow, weighed down with gold from the other two wagons. He swung into the saddle and trotted along, no longer worrying about an Aztec ambush. Something was wrong, terribly wrong.

He rode until the sun was high in the sky without finding a trace of Pitalpitoque, his warriors—or Angelina.

In frustration, Slocum called her name. The echoes rattled along the rocky walls and slowly faded. He'd used every trick he could think of to find her—or Pitalpitoque or the gold.

"Where are you, Angelina?" he called in growing anger. He was too good a tracker to have lost her and the others. And how could even a greenhorn miss a dozen men staggering under sacks of gold?

"Angelina!"

A single rock fell from the canyon rim, missing him by a few scant feet. Hand going for his Colt, Slocum went into a crouch and hunted for a target. He froze when he saw Pitalpitoque. The Aztec chief dangled from a high tree limb, an expression of stark horror etched on his dead face.

Turning, Slocum saw the rest of the Aztecs draped over limbs, all dead. The best he could tell, there wasn't a mark on any of them—and all had the same expression of unspeakable fear.

A second rock fell, forcing Slocum to look up the side of the cliff. It was sheer rock, no hidden Apache path here. At the top of the bluff, outlined against the sun, stood a figure he knew well.

"John Slocum, thank you!" Angelina called. She made a sweeping motion, sending a dozen gold coins cascading down around him. "Thank you!"

Before he could shout to her, the woman disappeared. In her place stood a tall man—or so it appeared to Slocum at first glance. But the sun shone off feathers and the movement was too sinuous, almost boneless. The person moved like a snake.

An arm raised, clutching an Aztec war club. From the other hand fell a single feather, floating down gently in defiance of the hot wind whistling and swirling along the valley. The solitary green feather landed softly at Slocum's feet.

It might have been the one he had found in the road so many weeks earlier, the one Angelina had taken from him. He picked it up and stroked along its silky, liquid length.

When he looked up again, even the second figure was gone.

"Good-bye, Angelina," Slocum said softly. He heaved a sigh. The gold was gone too, except for the handful of coins she had tossed him. He gathered them from the dust and put them into his saddlebags. Then he tucked the brilliant green feather into his hatband and said, "Good-bye, Quetzalcoatl."

Slocum rode north at last, determined to reach Santa Fe before he did something foolish—like going after Angelina and her feathered serpent protector.